WOMAN ON THE CROSS

ALSO BY PIERRE DELATTRE

WOMAN

on the CROSS

a novel by

Pierre Delattre

LOST HORSE PRESS   SANDPOINT   IDAHO

Library of Congress Cataloging in Publication Data

Delattre, Pierre, 1930-
Woman on the Cross: a novel/by Pierre Delattre.—1st ed.
p. cm.
ISBN 0-9668612-5-6 (alk. paper)
I. Title.
PS3554.E44 W66 2001
813'.54—dc21

First Edition

Cover Art by Lena Bartula
Design by Christine Holbert

Note: Throughout the book, the "j" in the correct Spanish spelling, *jilguero*, has been changed to an "h" to facilitate English pronunciation.

To all the women we men have martyred . . .

PART I

PROLOGUE

THOSE WHO KNOW the French language may have noted that the verb *seigner*, to bleed, remains connected to the name the French give to God and to Jesus Christ, and to the Lord above or below: *Seigneur*, the bleeder, Lord of the land (*Señor* in the Spanish language, shortened to *Sire* among the English); he who not only stands ready to shed his blood in protection of his people, but who reserves the right to shed the blood of the virgins.

Le droit du Seigneur, the right of the bleeder, was inexorably connected to the medieval divine right of kings. Fornication Under Command of the King, it was called among the Anglo-Saxons; or, to save time when the notice was sent to the girl's family, simply F.U.C.K.

In some of the French and Spanish feifdoms, it was considered a crime punishable by death for a girl to lose her virginity to anyone except the Lord her Bleeder, who not only guaranteed himself sexual pleasure free from the venereal diseases of that time, but also fathered enough bastard children so that a certain ambiguous loyalty was guaranteed among these whom he would favor with special privileges such as small grants of land and minor titles.

The supreme title, *Gran Señor*, Great Bleeder, was given so much honor among noblemen that inevitably it became confounded with the image of God's own relationship to the Holy Virgin. That was why the virgin doll in the glass case beside the baptismal font in the family chapel of the Cristo-Reys was reaching eagerly heavenward with arms open, and was wearing an enticing blue garter, her wedding dress partially pulled up. That was why the face of God painted on the hacienda's chapel ceiling bore such a likeness to one of the Cristo-Reys. Indeed, Sebastian's semblance or that of his father and his forefathers could be seen in just about every painting of God or of Christ on the ceilings and walls of the cathedrals, and on the holy images hung over the beds of the pious throughout the land.

As the feudal lords of the valley, as well as the men who, by profession, played the role of Jesus Christ in the great Holy Week festival held in whatever village or city the Cristo-Rey had chosen to honor that year, these men of the ancient and venerable guild of professional Christs regarded themselves as bound by a sacred contract with God Almighty to ritually enact the sexual union of God with the Holy Virgin. This springtime rite was to express God's yearning to plant his seed and to create his own image in man.

Not that the senior men of the Cristo-Rey confused themselves with God. They knew perfectly well that they were only vehicles for the divine drama, sinners like any priest. Each Cristo-Rey had been educated to caution the next generation against idolatry. The burden of piety would have been too heavy to bear if any of them had attempted to imitate the life of Christ. On the contrary, they saw themselves as playing a role that had precious little to do with their own personalities, and saw no contradiction in regaling their children with stories about their sometimes ribald behavior during their yearly visits to the place where—after the Holy Week drama had finally come to an end and, with their resurrection, they had declared that it was Easter—they were free to put on their civilian clothes, go out on the town with the mayor and the other dignitaries and have a rollicking good time, drinking, dancing and even somewhat purposefully debauching so as to remind those who saw them that the Cristo-Rey was a mere actor after all, not to be idolized or even treated with excessive veneration.

Even though some of the Cristo-Reys, according to the book

of records, had been exceedingly devout, others were equally famous for their profanity. In any case, it was only during certain highly sacramental rituals, such as during the Christ drama and during the bleeding of the bride, that God in some mysterious way was believed to take possession of them and to achieve his grand purpose despite and not because of who they happened to be on the plane of mortal eccentricity.

Sebastian had learned all this history from his father and now deceased grandfather on the day when he was taken up to the men's ceremonial lodge to receive the stigmata in the palms of his hands. It was the custom among the Cristo-Reys, as long as anyone could remember, for every male child to be stigmatized on his twelfth birthday. According to Sebastian's grandfather, there had been a time in the old country when the stigmata were placed in the feet as well as the hands. Old Amos Cristo-Rey liked to show the identical brown spots on each of his feet which he said were vestigial birthmarks of that ordeal. But Sebastian's father warned his son that his grandfather was an incorrigible mythmaker who liked to impress the ladies by glorifying the history of the Cristo-Reys, and that such boasts were unbecoming to the modesty of the family vocation.

In the ceremonial lodge, just before Amos and Abraham were to guide Sebastian through the ritual opening of his holy wounds (purification, chanting, holy inebriation and the surgery itself), Abraham reminded his trembling son that the wounds in his hands would be put there not so that he might experience Christ's pain, but that he might avoid it. Sebastian had already been cautioned by his sisters to let his hands be pierced without making a great hue and cry about it: to bear it like a man. They warned that he should be especially careful later on not to show off his wounds to the young women, which, of course, made him anticipate doing so all the more.

Sebastian had seen how attracted women were to his father's and grandfather's hands, wanting to kiss them whenever given the chance, which was frequently in Grandpa's case. Already, when he was a little boy, he knew that he would take after Grandpa because anything that had to do with arousing women aroused Sebastian.

At the dinner table when he was still a very little boy gazing with a frank and almost ardent fascination at Grandpa's gnarled old veiny fists, Sebastian felt certain, frightened as he was, that he would be more than willing to endure the pain of stigmatization. Like knotholes in an ancient tree they were, the scars around the edges of his grandfather's stigmata: thick and shiny and chocolate brown. Grandpa Amos had a way of throwing up his hands during dinner to express his delight. At such times, Sebastian could see clear through the leaf-shaped slits to the light from the window. He admired his father's wounds even more, but was embarrassed to stare at them since Abraham considered this bad manners. There were certain manzanita bushes up in the hills that had the same bright crimson scars as Sebastian saw on his father's hands. Inside the spike holes, the color was more purplish, and sometimes Abraham had to wear leather plugs, just as Sebastian did for the first years after his own stigmatization, to keep the holes from closing.

Abraham always wore gloves in public, even while dining in the village; though, during Holy Week, he was not adverse to removing a glove so that one of the Magdalenes, who were forever rushing to kneel and brush his father's feet with their hair, might enjoy the ecstasy of pressing her lips and tongue directly to the wound.

"Consider it." Abraham had said, speaking to his son for the first time in a man-to-man way as they walked up into the forest on the hill to the ceremonial lodge where Sebastian was to have his hands pierced. "For taking a few ceremonial wounds, we get to live in a style nobody else in this poor little country even dreams of. We're extravagantly paid for a few days work. Loved by the rich and the poor alike. Adored by our sisters and aunts: they spoil us rotten. Ours is the most joyous profession on earth. There's nothing to be afraid of except the possibility that they may take all this away from us. That's all I'm worried about. That's the real danger in the wind. Then we'd have to go out and work like everybody else. Why, I'd rather be crucified every month of the year than to have to give up this honored profession of ours."

He'd stopped and put his arm over Sebastian's shoulder as they turned to look down at the great valley with its flourishing fields, the hacienda there where the stream ran past, the pink dome of the chapel, the peach orchard, the vineyard with the workers busily pruning.

"I'm eternally grateful," he resumed as they continued their climb toward the lodge where old Amos had already fired up the stones for the sweat and prepared the table where Sebastian would lie after the smoke dance for the piercing of his hands. "I feel blessed that I was the first born so that at least I can do *something* honorable in this world. And I haven't begrudged our younger brothers the pure leisure they enjoy while we play the Christ. In fact, I pity them for not getting to be the ones who make the sacrifice. Nor do I begrudge them their enjoyments of the flesh."

He stopped again and gazed off with the same martyr's stare that Sebastian had seen him affect when he turned his face one last time sideways on the cross and, no longer looking down at the weeping women, glanced teary-eyed toward heaven.

Once your own son takes over the tupping, you too will accept your complete celibacy without complaint, knowing that during your days on the cross you enjoyed only the most beautiful of the virgins in the very way that God bequeathed his passion to the girl whom he so loved."

After his initiation, while the bandages were still on his hands and the pain was throbbing hard, Sebastian was shown the family book of records. It dated all the way back to the year

1114 in the village of La Bonne Vierge in southern France. From this book he learned that every *Grand Seigneur*, every crucified male, that is, sired eleven sons, and as many daughters as the brides he tupped happened to conceive before he retired into celibacy so as to avoid a twelfth son who, symbolizing Judas Iscariot, would have signalled a real death on the cross.

No Cristo-Rey had yet died during his acting out of the crucifixion, though they nearly became extinct on several occasions when almost all the sons died from the plague or from one wave of persecution or another. During the period of the Spanish Inquisition they were established in Spain where seven brave sons played the role of Christ in a single generation with true sacrifice, each being garrotted as a bastard and heretic because it had come out that they considered their original mother to be Mary Magdalene and their original father to be one whose name they would not speak, but whose identity certain accusers said they had claimed to be The Lord Jesus Himself.

Only the eighth and final Christ of the family's Spanish sojourn had somehow managed to defend himself against the charge of blasphemy with sufficient success so that the court of The Escorial spared him, merely sending him across the ocean into exile.

While Sebastian's family book indicated that the Cristo-Reys lived in rather dire straights for several generations in their new land—being nothing more than gypsy players—a time came when rumors they had spread about the true origin of the blackened old cross they carried strapped to the roof of their wagon finally passed through the folklore into the secure realm of established fact. Crucifixion became a lucrative business again. Finally, the Cristo-Reys were given their fertile valley as a land grant from a government grateful for all the tourism they brought to the country.

In the meantime, they had remained so healthy that only

one or two sons from each generation of Christs ever went to the cross, though all eleven continued to receive the stigmata. The uncrucified ones no longer had to beg, borrow and steal for a living, but were able to enjoy lives of leisure, as Sebastian's brothers did, being pampered at home by their many sisters and aunts. A tradition developed that they would leave home as soon as their oldest brother yielded the cross to his son; and none of Sebastian's uncles had failed to do so, for they had all been eager to take the settlement they received from their brother's sumptuous earnings as the Christ and to go off somewhere to fulfil their longings finally to marry and have children of their own. They almost never came home to visit the senior Cristo-Rey after that. At the same time, the sisters of these men, who were prematurely exhausted from sensual deprivation and from having had to wait hand and foot on the men of the household for so many years were only too happy to exercise their right to depart the hacienda for a convent where they remained cloistered until death.

As long as their oldest brother was still going to the cross, the younger sons of the retired Cristo-Rey were not allowed to marry, though they could sport with as many women as they wished, providing they did not have to take up the role of Christ (as seldom happened). Sebastian's brothers, therefore, knew nothing of marital love, but only of brief, wild, passionate flings that usually ended with the woman in question being abandoned for someone more fresh and exciting.

The bastard men and the women of the family—that is to say all the children born of the brides of Christ—were forbidden by etiquette from even inquiring about who their mothers might be, though it was not too hard to guess since she had to be one of the daughters of those men who had been freed from serfdom and given land of their own. When one of the men or women of the Cristo-Reys was riding through the valley, he or she often stopped to gaze at women doing their work in the yards or in the fields, or rode along beside them when passing them as they drove cattle or carried water along the road, and wondered which one might be his or her mother. The woman in question would not have dared give any sign, since that was considered a grave criminal offence to be punished in ways unspeakable.

The only lasting love a Christ-actor of the Cristo-Reys knew anything about in relation to women was the love he received as a child from his aunts, his sisters, and later from his daughters—fruits of the wombs he had laid claim to.

Now that we have seen how it was with the family of the Cristo-Reys at the time when Sebastian first took up the cross, our story can begin.

O N E

THE SEVEN SISTERS and nine aunts of Sebastian
Cristo-Rey hung bird cages under the arches of the patio,
hung them from spikes driven into the walls, hung them in the
lemon trees, hung them in their bedroom windows, from their
balconies, and even sometimes carried them about through
the corridors, a cage swinging in each hand so that wherever
they stopped to sit and talk or read or dream they could have
music. Some cages spun when the wind blew hard, and other
cages swayed from the hopping of a bird from one perch to
another.

The singing of the birds only stopped when the hoods were
placed over their cages at night. In the morning, even before
going to chapel, the women, as their first and favorite household chore, took the covers off the cages, cajoling the male
birds with cheerful whistling into resuming their song.

When he heard the birds begin to sing, Sebastian always felt
a gladness in his throat that made him want to cry out with
happiness. He would throw the covers off his own bed and run
outside to greet the day.

Nobody had told him when he was young, and he still found
it hard to believe now that he was a man already enacting his
sacred vocation as Christ, that all he had been hearing was the
birds' distress. He had taken their songs for the music of joy.

From his aunt, Maria Latona, who knew so many things,
Sebastian learned very late why the songbirds really sing.

"They sing for loneliness," she said. "Didn't you know that,
Cristo-Rey? Didn't you know those birds all sing because their
mates are locked away in cages they can never hope to reach?
Those are the males that you hear sing, and you won't hear

their loveliest song unless you put the female birds that they most ardently desire close to them in another cage where they can see her. Try it. Put her so close that he can even smell the scent her tail wafts to him when she fans it up and down. Then listen to how desperately he sings."

"He sings because he's *happy*," Sebastian insisted, scratching his beard to remind himself he was no longer the boy he always felt he was in the presence of Maria Latona. But he couldn't resist reaching across the table, as he had when he was a boy, and scraping around the bowl until the sugary dough had made a nice thick whirl at the top of his finger.

"No, no, my boy. Each male only sings for grief. He sings because of his great longing to have her with him under his wings. Take her cage away, you'll see. He'll stop. Hang the cage again nearby, his song resumes."

Sebastian sucked the dough from his finger and shook his head.

Believe me," she insisted. "These birds of the hacienda are dying for love. And when they've sung their hearts out, what happens to them? Tell me."

Sebastian looked over his shoulder through the kitchen door at the cages that dangled from the rafters along the patio corridor. Every brightly plumed male had his more lackluster female in another cage close by. He said, "I don't know."

"You've seen them on the bottom of the cage with their feet in the air. They fall off their perch and drop down dead."

Despite terrible revelations like this, Sebastian liked Maria Latona. He imagined that his mother (wherever she was) had to be a large breasted matronly sort—a real peasant woman, huge like this—to have carried a boy who grew up to be as tall and powerful as he was. In a sense, all his more buxom aunts, through the wishing of it, were the mother Sebastian did not really have.

This one aunt was rolling dough, stretching her plump body across the long wooden table while she brought her weight down on the rolling pin, plunging back and forth in front of him so that he could smell the satisfying sweat of her breasts while she told him the story of the birds, how they sang only because they were lonely.

"Without the female in another cage nearby, it's impossible for them to sing."

"And if the two are placed inside the same cage, what then?"

Maria Latona stopped rolling the dough. She stood up straight, thought it over and shrugged. "Sometimes they sing a little bit. But not the true distress song we humans like to hear. Sometimes they sing a pretty song when they've been reunited, but not that special song which thrills you to the heart."

She placed her flour-whitened hand on her bosom, looked out through the doorway into the peach orchard: "For them to sing their hearts out, nephew dear, they have to weep down deep in their throats. It may be a terrible thing to say, but you'll never hear them warble so beautifully out there among the trees. That is surely something you men of the Cristo-Rey are bound to learn."

"What's that?"

Sebastian felt a quick stab of pain in both his hands where just a week ago he had endured his first time being nailed to the cross.

"Why, suffering can always be heard in the prettiest of songs. It's when he can't have the girl he desires that a boy lets out the beauty in his soul. I suppose you've learned already that the Cristo-Reys lose the power of song once they've been crucified. They can never sing after that in the way of the true singers of this land, the troubadours. Oh, you may have sung some pretty little ditties when you were still a virgin to the cross, but you're a saviour now. Singing won't come so easy now that you've gone to heaven," she chuckled somewhat bitterly, "*and* come back better than ever, mind you, ready to gobble down your Aunt Latona's sweet rolls while they're still good and hot."

Sebastian smiled, not letting Maria Latona know how she had wounded him. His father had warned him that he must accept and forgive the resentment always lurking under the surface among the women of the family.

"Because of my crucifixion, I can no longer sing?"

"Of course not, my dear boy. Not beautifully. Haven't you been listening to what I say? Once you can ravish any little virgin lamb you choose, the beauty's lost. Am I right or wrong?"

Sebastian didn't understand. He felt like a child again. He slid off his stool and walked in a sulk out of the kitchen, shouting over his shoulder, "Well then, I hope I have eleven sons in just as many years so that I can put down the cross while I'm still in my thirties."

"Oh, once you've played the Christ," Maria Latona shouted after him, with a satisfaction she made no effort to conceal, "the singing's gone forever, I'm afraid."

He ambled out between the barns and up into the orchard, whistling, clapping his hands to startle the birds from the trees. He sang at the top of his voice, wildly, ecstatically, warbling, it seemed to him, as beautifully as any of the birds in their cages.

After a while, however, something broke in his voice. He had reached for a very high note, but a deeper sound, hoarse and ugly came out of his throat instead. He stopped singing and wandered on back to the kitchen, feeling strangely perturbed.

Aunt Maria Latona had cut and folded the dough. With a canister under her arm, she was sticking raisins into the center of each pastry.

"Well, you do sing up quite a storm," she snickered. "You're a real match for the jays and the blackbirds."

"Come now, Auntie," Sebastian laughed. "Put aside that bitterness all you women of our household have some need to put in everything you say. Be as sweet as your breads and tarts and admit the truth. There's not a single bird that sings more beautifully than I do."

"Oh, my señor, of course I can't think of a one."

She tilted her head, listening to a memory. "Except the *hilguero*, of course."

Maria Latona cackled in a way that made her eyes turn into slits. "Excuse me, Sebastian, but in all honesty I have to tell you that *Hilguero* sings the sweetest song of all. I mean, when he suffers. And his suffering, it's not just acted out, if you'll forgive my saying so, the way you Cristo-Reys pretend to act out God's own suffering on the cross."

She placed her hands under her breasts, lifted them, closed her eyes and heaved a sigh. "When *Hilguero* sings most beautifully, you know his suffering belongs to him. It's his very own."

Maria Latona opened her eyes, seemed startled, removed her hands from her breasts, moved her hands swiftly to the cuts of dough on the table, and began to fold the corners over the raisins.

"I thought I knew the names of all the birds," Sebastian said. "But I've never heard of any *hilguero*. Which one is he?"

"*Hilguero?* We don't have him in any of our cages. No. *Hilguero's* song causes him too much pain for any of us women, even your sisters, to take much pleasure in hearing it." She wet her lips with her tongue. "Except at the time of sacrifice when all you men of the Cristo-Rey are off to the crucifixion. Then we have the hacienda all to ourselves, and we make a great feast."

"You have a feast while I'm not here?"

"While none of you noble men or boys are here, young Sire. Indeed we do." She looked about to make sure no ghost or invisible person was listening, and continued in a quieter voice:

"So that this feast will be especially joyous, one of our servant men goes out into the hills high up above the snow line in the pines, and he traps the blue *hilgueros*, the male and female together. They aren't hard to catch. All you do is put some berries in a box and set the stick to make the trap door fall. Both male and female come to feed together. You seldom catch one without catching the other. But, if you bring them home and leave them in that single cage, they won't sing, of course. He'll hop about taking positions to defend her, pecking at your finger. Look, see?"

She rubbed away a circle of flour on the back of her hand and showed him the little scar. "Right here is where he bled me. Oh, he can be vicious defending her. While she sits there perched in the center of the cage, he'll hop all around her, up and down, from floor to ceiling, perch to perch. He'll hop and hop while she just sits there blinking her eyes."

"But he won't sing?"

"No, he won't sing."

Maria Latona went to fetch a tray, rubbed lard over it, and set the rolls upon it. As in his boyhood, when hanging about the kitchen so that he could be near to the most motherly women, Sebastian ran to open the big iron doors of the oven. Inside, the bricks flashed with blue flame. An aroma of orange peels, cinnamon and raisin blew a hot gust of his aunt's bread pudding into the kitchen. She thrust the tray onto one of the racks.

"But if . . ." she said.

He shut the oven for her. They walked out onto the patio to cool off.

"If what?"

"If you put her in another cage just a few yards away, that's a different matter. Oh, I tell you, after that he'll sing until you think your heart is going to burst for joy. On the night when all our brothers and nephews are off with Father at the resurrection, we bring *Hilguero* and his mate into the courtyard; and while he sings we dance, we tell stories, we laugh, we feast."

"With whom do you dance? Feast?"

The image of his aunts and sisters carousing with men amused Sebastian, for they were all virgins—at least as far as he knew. They were like nuns, sworn to celibacy all their lives, these women who called themselves *The Sisters of the Cristo-Rey* and wore habits of blue that hid their flesh from neck to toe.

"Promise you won't tell?"

"Tell whom? I'm the Christ now. I don't need to tell anybody anything."

"All right. I know you're not like some of the Cristo-Reys who begrudge us women our few episodes of fun. What we do is this: we invite the wandering singers. The troubadours. Or, to put it more bluntly, as soon as they know you're gone they swarm down from the hills in droves."

"They come down to the hacienda? What for? Father doesn't fancy their performances."

"Oh, but we women do. They come to sport with us, and I mean not just with your sisters. Your old aunties get plenty of action too, believe you me."

She smoothed her hands up and down her thighs and gave off a long, somewhat obscene groan.

Sebastian blushed, he was so shocked. "But you don't . . ."

"No, we maintain our purity, mind you. That's what makes it so sweet. The pain of coming so close and yet not yielding up what we still hold most precious."

Hiding his displeasure so as to hear more, Sebastian grinned. "And you have all this fun while the *hilguero* sings?"

"Yes, but the trouble, you see, is that, while *Hilguero* sings, his mate starts to thrash about. She's so furious to be separated from him that she goes absolutely wild. Within a few hours, she's dead from beating her wings against the bars of the cage. Her feathers go flying, the poor thing. Sometimes she breaks a wing. And when she's dead his singing stops after one last final trill of pain . . ."

Aunt Maria Latona turned her gaze up sideways, looking out through the door to the open sky, in a way that reminded Sebastian of the gesture his father had made when, on the cross, he said his *Lama Sabachtani*, and gave up the ghost.

". . . A warbling so beautiful to hear that everyone puts down their drinks. We pause to listen. We smile, embrace. And then, when the *hilguero's* singing stops, something possesses all of us. Even us older ones long to be embracing with a mate. The death of that poor female bird makes us all yearn to be together in the mating cage."

Tears filled her eyes, whether from happiness or sorrow, Sebastian could not tell.

"The death of that poor bird quickens something in our bodies. When the male *hilguero* sings his final grief, watching his lady lying there on the bottom of the cage, don't you know? Already so stiff and cold? That's when the men go wild for us. That's when they most courteously but insistently escort us to our beds."

"Then you *do* . . ."

"Almost. Oh, it's delicious the way we torture those lovers of ours. And the way they torture *us*."

She leaned against an arch, held her stomach, and chuckled deep inside herself.

"And while you torment each other with what you cannot have," Sebastian said evenly, hiding his disgust, "does the male die too?"

She threw back her head and shrieked. "Listen, Sebastian. You think you've had a taste of God's exquisite agony up there on your precious cross. But I can tell you of one young fellow whom I put in agony—a fine singer he was, more Christ than you, if nobility of spirit, forgive me, counts for anything. This lover of mine lost his voice for a full month, the way I made his staff stand up. Raised him so high in ecstasy, I don't think he's come down yet. Next year when they take you down, you won't even be a virgin any longer. What kind of Christ is that, really? We *Sisters of the Cristo-Rey* keep our lovers hanging there until the shine in their eyes is so bright with pure and unrelieved desire that I'm quite sure from then on they have no trouble seeing in the dark."

"This is all too strange," Sebastian said.

"We're not like other families, young man. Nothing like them at all."

"We torment our flesh," Sebastian sighed.

"We know more ecstasy," she said. "And we know more pain. Like the *hilguero*."

"And does the male *hilguero* also die while you and these troubadours of yours are tormenting each others' flesh that way?"

"Oh, yes," she nodded solemnly, "indeed he does."

"You enjoy it, then? Being nearly ravished while the *hilgueros* die?" He was suddenly breathless. He felt his heart beating fast. The cords in his neck tightened. "Why don't you actually bed down with these troubadours? Lose your precious virginity. Stop torturing yourselves."

Maria Latona staggered back, hands on her hips. "What a thing to suggest! Be tupped like some common bride of the Cristo-Rey?"

She wiped the flour off her hands down across her breasts and stomach onto her apron. She looked at Sebastian with astonishment.

"The *real thing* men do to women when they pierce their flesh . . . never! I would never want to do the real thing. Then all is lost. Then and thenceforth, life is pure pain devoid of ecstasy. Life is pure hell after that."

"You call it hell to be possessed by a man? What of the brides I'll tup?"

Maria Latona snorted. "What of them?" She laughed miserably and crossed herself three times. "God save the wretched children."

Sebastian didn't know what to say. He had it in his head that when the bleeder of the virgins, whom he was next in line to be, lies with the lucky girl, she must be as delirious with joy as when the virgin Mary pulls up her wedding dress and abandons herself to the lust of the Holy Spirit.

Hearing his aunt talk this way, Sebastian wondered for the first time whether there was as much rapture with the bleeding of a bride as his brothers had led him to believe.

He would soon find out.

The tupping of his first bride was to take place in only a few more days. At the thought of all those virgin girls in bridal gowns lined up for his inspection, he felt a tingling of his sex, but then a withering sensation that made him look away from Maria Latona down to the wounds that were still palpitating in his hands.

ON THE FIRST DAY in May, following a night when the moon was dark, all the girls in the valley who were to be married that year were dressed up in bridal gowns and brought to the chapel on the hacienda of the Cristo-Reys so that one of them might be chosen as the bride of Christ. It was then, as they stood lined up in the sun, that the senior Cristo-Rey, The Bleeder, traditionally walked out in his finery, and chose.

The first year that Sebastian Cristo-Rey chose a bride, he was already 27 with no experience whatsoever, for the eldest son of the Cristo-Reys was vowed to celibacy except with the brides of Christ during the years when he played the role of saviour, and he would never have dreamed of breaking this vow. He was certain that he would die and go straight to hell if he should ever allow himself sexual intercourse with any woman except a virgin, and only a virgin in the first year of her womanhood. She must be the girl that he himself had chosen, according to the custom of his family for centuries, by lifting the veil and looking into her face on the day when it was finally his turn to play the Christ, which also meant his turn henceforth, until he relinquished the privilege to his son, each day in May when the brides lined up in front of the chapel to select the girl he wanted for the planting of his seed.

That night would be his only chance with her. She would stay at the hacienda, cared for by his sisters, until he learned whether or not he had made her pregnant. If she bled at the next full moon (in those days, at least in the valley of the Cristo-Rey, women's menstrual cycles were known to be caused by the fullness of the moon), she would return home;

but if she became pregnant she stayed at the hacienda until the child was born and could be turned over to a wet nurse, at which time her father would come to claim his reward: release from serfdom and a substantial land grant in the valley. He would be allowed to return his daughter to a normal though more comfortable life at home, presumably involving marriage and more children, none of which was to be of concern to Sebastian.

Yes, Sebastian was frightened that first time. He had endured his initial crucifixion only a week before. The experience had been much more shattering to his nerves than he had imagined. He was haunted by the faces of all those women in black wringing their hands and lamenting with shrieks and wails at the foot of his cross, and he was also still weak from the ordeal, the tendons across his shoulders and ribs inflamed and tender. Even though he had looked forward to his night with the bride for such a long time, having endless fantasies about it, playing out variations on how he would enjoy her, now that the time had come, he felt as if something inside of him was bleeding and that she and he were both doomed to a night of pain.

He didn't pick the loveliest one; her eyes were too defiant. Nor did he pick the one who seemed to want him most, seeing that she would know more than he did about what to do. He did not want to appear inept.

He was afraid to choose the terrified one because he knew that they would both lie down shaking and sweating against each other, and that they might disgrace themselves by failing to conceive a child. So he picked one whose rather slouched posture suggested docility.

She shrugged when he touched her shoulder. When he lifted her veil, she lowered her eyes. His father was surprised that Sebastian would choose one whose face was so homely, but Sebastian didn't care. In truth, her homeliness added to his confidence.

"Jesus was a beautiful man," Abraham Cristo-Rey admonished

after Sebastian had returned to the veranda and the brides had begun to file into the chapel for communion. "Do you want to make an ugly Christ?"

Sebastian was not obliged to answer; and he didn't. He himself was the Christ now. Having begun his retirement, the elder Cristo-Rey was not supposed to impose his judgements upon the son.

Sebastian took her limp hand in his that evening when her proud peasant father handed her over to him. Sebastian led her, almost dragged her, to the chapel. They stood in the chancel facing each other. He took hold of both her hands. He saw in the dim candle glow that her eyes were still lowered. She had not looked at him once. They just stood there in the dusk waiting for something to happen.

When he could see through the round window above the cross that it was pitch black outside, he let go of her and went to blow out all the candles on the altar but a single one. Then he asked her to lie down upon the straw spread there on the tiles beneath the cross. She did so without objection, turning her horsy face meekly aside.

He sat down beside her. She let him pull her skirt up. She spread her legs the moment he rested a hand on her thigh. She let him undo her bodice, without struggle, breathing heavily, but not complaining, her eyes shut tight.

She let him kiss her nipples, though he could hardly discern the little bumps with his lips. To the tip of his tongue, they were icy cold. Nothing that his mouth or tongue attempted could warm them or make them swell, as his younger brothers (womanizers all) had told him they would. Her mouth stayed pursed when he took her chin in his hand and touched his lips to it. Nor could he, as he had been so often told to do, push in his tongue even to the point of touching her teeth.

When he laid his hand on the small nest of silky curled hair between her legs, he felt no moisture there. He undid himself, climbed on top of her and, being very hard, managed to press the lips of her womanhood apart, but just a little. Before he could penetrate very deeply, he spilled his seed. Then he heard himself give off a long moan that echoed off the walls and vaults of the chapel, sounding like the ghost of a lonely child. She hadn't made a sound.

He felt dejected. Somewhat angrily, he pulled her dress down.

She said, "Is it over?"

"Yes," he said. And she was gone.

His brothers had to go out in search of her that night. They finally found her up in the orchard, and brought her back to the house where she stayed in her room, even eating there, and refusing to see him. He didn't care to see her either. He was sure that in a few weeks she would prove not to be pregnant and would be sent on her way. But when he found out that she was indeed going to have a child, he was surprised at how eager he was to be with her. She eventually agreed to let him come up and have supper with her.

Though she pouted and pretended to pay no attention to his endearments, he eventually did manage to get a bit of scornful laughter out of her with profane stories he was later ashamed to remember telling, about amusing things that happened to him on the path to the cross. He felt genuinely sad when she was taken back to the farm by her father after being delivered of a girl child.

While he was standing in an upstairs room of the hacienda, watching the cart rattle off across the cobblestones with the father's arm over his daughter's shoulder, the girl's head turning back and forth against the man's neck as if she were grinding away at her grief, Sebastian's own father suddenly strode up behind him and seized him by the shoulders.

"Well now, my man," Abraham said gruffly, "let's make a *son* next time, shall we?"

"I'll certainly try, father," Sebastian heard himself murmur.

Abraham gave off a snort. He slammed a knee into

Sebastian's buttocks. "That's too weak an attitude. You're not playing a meek and gentle Jesus any more, not when it comes to the tupping. You're playing Lord and Master. God on High did not wish for the creation of the world. He made it happen through his will and might. To make a son, you have to approach it with vigor, lad. You have to go at it with tremendous longing. Generate the power of the universe. Go after the next one as if the redemption of humankind depended on it. A deep plunge is best. Thorough ravishment."

Sebastian promised he would approach the task more fiercely.

THREE

H E S E I Z E D the next bride by the hair and threw her down beneath the altar. She struggled like an animal about to be slaughtered, escaping from him while he tore at her clothes. He had to chase her around inside the chapel, up into the choir loft, around the pews, all the way up to the belfry where he caught her by the ankle just before she jumped from the rail, brought her thumping onto her back, raped her right there, then carried her half unconscious down the winding stairs to the altar and raped her again.

The pleasure he felt from this did not last an instant beyond that second time he spent his seed. For months afterward, he suffered a remorse that made it difficult for him even to look up at the cross during his family's daily morning devotions in the chapel.

Nevertheless, he raped the next bride too; and the next, though both of them, stiff and tearful, offered no resistance except when, during his own involuntary whimpering, he pried their legs apart. Not one of them became pregnant by him. He hated each one more for the way the one before her had failed him. And it was clear to him that the more he hated the more hate was returned to him. Among the girls in the valley, perhaps among their families too, he knew that he had become certainly the most hated and despised of all the Cristo-Reys.

He also knew what the men in their families were thinking from the subtly mocking way they tipped their hats to him when he went out riding. How could he expect to be called a Sire when he did not even know how to pass his manhood through the bleeding flesh of a woman with sufficient power for the planting of his seed? He was mocked and despised by the peasants, and he didn't blame them because he secretly felt the same way about himself. It had begun to affect his behavior when he went to the cross. His manner had become ever more humble, almost apologetic. Not that this affected his popularity. On the contrary, the populace was happy to have a modest Christ with more appearance of inner piety after the years of rather arrogant performance by Sebastian's father.

Sebastian knew with a certain bitterness toward himself that he was a great crowd pleaser in showing a kind of humble forbearance during his trial; an inner reserve as he walked up the hill to Calvary; a laconic indifference to his crucifixion; and what aficionados called his exquisitely executed resurrection from the tomb on the third day.

He was quite certain that he would not be so universally loved by the weeping Marys, out there away from the village of the Cristo-Reys, if the inability of the man who played Christ to arrive at any notion of carnal affection between a man and a woman became known, for the linking of love with sexual union was, as he learned from his sisters, a new idea, very much in the air.

From his sisters, he began to get an inkling of how that kind of love might be possible. It was from the old songs of the troubadours, sung by the women of his house, that Sebastian first learned of courtly romance.

Amor, an old, old word on the continent, had only just arrived in the New World. When Sebastian's father heard of it, he said that love meant the love of God for man and man for God. Love was an expression of spirituality, quite outside the bodily world. He laughed at love as far as courtship was concerned. Love transcended our bodily nature. Love was a soulful passion he had felt most intensely when stretched out upon the cross. As for a woman's love for a man, this was to be expressed by her complete devotion. Such a love was exemplified by the sacrifice his sisters made by not marrying and remaining celibate so that they could be at home to make life comfortable for him; it meant the love the Mary Magdalenes had felt for him, the ones who had liked to weep at the foot of his cross, the ladies who had pleaded every year to be the ones to anoint his body with oil, to wash his feet with their hair, even to anoint him after he had come down from the cross; those Magdalenes who had begged to let them wrap him up for death, who had stayed near the tomb to weep so that he could take comfort, hearing them through the stone. Many were the women whose love Abraham Cristo-Rey sorely missed, whom he envied Sebastian for enjoying such intimacy with, now that Sebastian had taken over the role of Christ.

Abraham saw nothing of that sublime kind of love in the bestial act whereby a man and a woman were compelled to couple sexually. Nor could his son comprehend how such love might be possible or even relevant during those first years, especially when every girl who was bled at Sebastian's command left him feeling more desolate. Every bride brought him closer to the time when (he was certain of it now) he would have to relinquish the Christ role to his younger brother Roman and suffer the rest of his life in shame.

"Maybe you'd have better luck if you deflowered your little bride with just a touch of amorousness," his oldest sister whispered to him one evening as he stood on the porch of the hacienda, looking out at where the brides would line up next May.

FOUR

AT THE INSTIGATION of his sisters, Sebastian invited a band of troubadours from the capital city to come live at the hacienda and to bring poetry and music to its halls. The troubadours knew nothing of the actual physical act of love between a man and a woman, but only the longing for it. They preferred to court the very women they could not possess. They espoused the *via negativa*, the way of denial, teaching what they called "the spiritual art of love," which was to bring carnal desire to its peak, to arouse the flesh only so that sexual ardor might be transmuted into an ardor for God. Among the aristocracy of the land, they had been much in demand as teachers of a kind of lovemaking that did not actually involve the penetration of the woman by the man, perhaps not so much because of the troubadours' conception of transforming physical into spiritual love as because venereal disease had become so epidemic that alternative means were being sought.

These troubadours, as Sebastian already knew from his Aunt Maria Latona, were exactly the men *The Sisters of the Cristo-Rey* longed to be with. Indeed, since their arrival at the hacienda, the women of the house had ceased to appear so grey and prematurely aged. They had changed the style of the garment they wore from one resembling a nun's habit to a much more attractive, though simple, yellow dress. They were not averse to wearing crowns of wild flowers picked for them by their lovers. Their faces had begun to shine with a delirious kind of happiness, and Sebastian was often thrilled by the very sweetness of their flesh, a pungent, exciting odor they exuded sometimes after being entertained by their lovers. Sebastian himself began to wish that he could spend time with the troubadours, and looked for excuses to do so.

He persuaded the most charming and sought after among them, Talifiero his name was, to teach him the rudiments of harp playing, which Talifiero was happy to do, taking the opportunity to instruct Sebastian on some simple tricks of versification. It was in a kind of rapture he had never known a man could feel that he went to the chapel every night before bed time, knelt there where he had bled his bride, and thanked God for showing him how those who love the one they lie with receive what they desire.

He begged God to forgive him for the way he had so cruelly injured his brides.

Deep remorse began to show in his demeanor. It gave him a kind of beauty that made the women out there in the larger world wild with desire for him. His contrite expression seemed to evoke their bliss.

The next Good Friday, in a hot village on the coast, Sebastian Cristo-Rey chose to hang on the cross longer than any Christ before him. He tried to stay up there in the hot sun of Calvary, nailed to the cross twice as long as Jesus Christ Himself; and he almost died on account of it.

Sebastian told the centurions not to take him down until he had suffered at least six hours. Thanks, if truth be told, to the addition on the cross of a wooden bar on which he could slightly rest his buttocks, he managed not to let the powerful muscles of his arms and shoulders quite yield; his rib cage was only torn and never actually broken. But he came down very afflicted in the chest. After his three nights in the tomb, he emerged as pale as a ghost. He had to be taken home wrapped in blankets, delirious, sweating and freezing. The pain from almost having his lungs collapse seemed to affect the quiet of his heart. He started having seizures. Strange emotions followed him at night like ghosts pursuing. He would run away from them, howling from his room, down the porch of the hacienda and out into the orchard, pulling at his hair.

He was too sick to tup one of the brides that May. He stayed in bed. Abraham found his son kneeling in the chapel a few days later, wailing out his grief. Abraham walked down the aisle of the nave up into the chancel.

"For shame, Sebastian. Quiet down. A Cristo-Rey does not conduct himself like this in front of the family cross."

He placed a hand on Sebastian's head, and ruffled his hair.

"We aren't all born to this vocation, lad. Isn't it time you passed the cross to your brother Roman?"

BUT HOW COULD Sebastian pass the cross on to Roman, whom Father had not even bothered to take into his spiritual confidences?

It's not that I wasn't born to the vocation of Christ, Sebastian had wanted to shout at his father. It's that no Christ wants to be born for me. But, of course, his father knew that. He was simply being discrete. He could not say, You haven't the virility to be a senior Cristo-Rey. You lack the powers of the bleeder. It would have been too demeaning to say, God has not blessed your body with the knowledge of how to make a son.

"But what if it was not me?" Sebastian said to the cross under which he still knelt long after his father had gone away. "What if the weakness was all with the brides? What if it was entirely their fault, and not mine at all?"

(Those brides who appeared to him at night like white robed harpies, hallucinations that mocked him.)

"They fly around my bed defying me to plant the seed I know I have here burning in my loins. The seed of a Christ even greater than I."

As for passing the cross on to his brother?

"How could I let myself even think of it? I must find a way not to let that happen. Why, Roman's only good for getting drunk and seducing women. Even on Holy Week when all the town's sunk into spiritual darkness, my brother is somewhere down there in the blackest room of all. I know he goes out hunting for the most pious ones, the women who love me most. Oh, Lord god and Father, I see how he takes one by her black gloved hand. He pulls her along through some dark alley, drags her into the back room or some tavern or brothel. I see him push this woman onto a bed. So pious and solemn she is about it. I see him laying back the shadows of her dress. While her thoughts are still on me, he lifts her skirt; he presses his mouth to her pale thigh. His wine-stinking mouth. Oh, the pleasure he must take when she succumbs. Sometimes it seems to me my brothers have no other purpose in life than to take revenge on me for being Lord among the Cristo-Reys. They're like my shadows. And Roman is the darkest shadow of them all. He's good only for dressing up like a centurion and driving the spikes into my hands.

"Roman hasn't read The Gospels. He knows more about his last mistress than about Jesus Christ. Roman would disgrace a great tradition. He'd stumble to the cross drunk, leering at the Magdalenes all the way up to Calvary. If Roman took on the role, the mob wouldn't just pretend to mock and revile him; they'd be quite serious about it. They might even stone him to death out of sheer rage for having to watch such a scoundrel play the role of God."

There was no doubt about it. For Roman's own sake, Sebastian must find a way to make a son. If he could not make the miracle happen from his own loins, then he must contrive another way.

"Besides," Sebastian said the next morning to his image in the mirror. "Look at me. I'm the one blessed with a Christ-like appearance. What would the women think of Roman with his nose so flattened by the punches he's taken in tavern brawls? The women who adore me so."

Sebastian wondered too how he could ever bear to forsake the exhilaration brought to him by the sorrow of the weeping women. No, he would not give up the cross. And next Good Friday he would make the women weep a veritable river of tears.

As, indeed, they did.

SIX

THE NEXT YEAR at his crucifixion, the women wept for Sebastian in droves, thousands upon thousands in their mourning gowns, their black dresses and their blacker veils, their black stockings and their black shoes, these women all in black, not just from the little country of the Cristo-Reys, but from all over the world, women arriving to the crucifixion by boat and carriage, sometimes even on foot from far off places, having heard about the man who suffered twice as long as Christ, wanting to see him, wanting to be right there at the foot of his cross, willing to pay great sums to be allowed close enough to stroke his feet with their hair and to kiss his wounds, or at least buy one of the expensive kneeling places close enough to the cross so that he would hear them weep and perhaps favor them with a direct gaze from his hugely troubled eyes.

The money these women spent during Holy Week enriched the country and brought a magnificent honorarium to Sebastian. These sometimes very wealthy women made a fabulous horde. There must have been ten thousand come to see him die on the cross; and all were wailing loudly while he hung there turning his beautiful profile to heaven, his long, sensuous, caramel hair blowing up in a twirl around the stem of the cross as he lowered his gaze occasionally to show the women that he knew they were there suffering with him, *for* him, desiring whatever it was of him that was in agony.

They wailed the hysteria of their love up to him while he hung there, his long, sinuous, shining torso covered only by the scantiest of cloths, one knee crossed over the other, and that particular turn of his hip that was just feminine enough to make them feel that they were sharing his pain in some excruciatingly exciting way.

They forgot that he was a mere actor. Perhaps for the first time in history, these women worshipped a Cristo-Rey for his own sake.

He had to confess to himself that he encouraged their idolatry. He was provoking them to the worship of none other than the confused man (the impotent man) from the valley of the Cristo-Reys. Yes, he knew that. And, to atone for what he knew was his great sin, he worked hard to be more worthy than any professional Christ before him of carrying that great length of wood up the steep hill to Calvary.

After his resurrection that year, he did not attend the more effete parties to mix with courtly gentlemen. He sought the admiration of the more virile working men of the town, the ones he suspected of despising him for his attractiveness to their women. He allowed his brothers to drag him off to an arena where the men who worked at the various butcher shops were holding their annual wrestling contest. He was amazed with himself, and so were all the men in the crowd, when they saw the Christ strip off his shirt and climb into the ring to take on one who had been the victor thus far, a brute who called himself The Azteca.

Drawing on all the reserves he had gathered during three nights resting in the tomb, Sebastian managed to throw The Azteca out of the ring.

Oh, it was good to get drunk after that, to stand with the other brutes: oafishly unbuttoning his fly and emptying his bladder against the tiles of the tavern bar, sharing his stink, watching his piss swirl down the open, steaming trough into the drain with the dark yellow piss of all the others. And to have his brothers and all the butcher boys wanting to buy him another round, wanting to pat him on the back so that they could feel the power in his shoulders. Best of all, to have that stinking, wonderfully cheerful animal called The Azteca mooning over him while needing to stand close to him like any woman.

As soon as he returned home, Sebastian began to organize athletic contests with his brothers and wasn't satisfied until he could beat them all at running or jumping or hurling the spear or heaving heavy stones. He rode, he ran, he wrestled with the strongest peasants in the fields. Lately, he had begun to affect the swagger of a champion, especially at home among the courtiers of his sisters, whom he had come to despise.

The troubadours lived for the fun of the moment and called it living for God. They claimed that the body is like a cup that must be filled with erotic passion so that God can come drink from it in the night.

What a blasphemous simile, his father said, during one of their ever more infrequent conversations in the privacy of Abraham's study.

"Who is this God who requires their effeminate passion for His sustenance? Is it not quite the opposite with God?" Abraham asked. "If a man can only worship God by adoring women, then he must secretly hate God. And if he can only love women by adoring the image of God he finds in them, then he must secretly hate women, at least in their mere mortal aspect.

"Whatever the case," Abraham warned his son, "beware of these idolaters. Whether they hate or revile God, they will make you too womanish for the kind of ordeal we men of the Cristo-Rey must undergo when we are face to face with *our* God on the cross. You may have proved your physical prowess, but I can see plainly that you want to worship women. You want to take their softness into yourself. That is not our way. I tell you again, harden yourself to the challenge. It's a manly one. The mob loves us, but the mob hates us too. Show any weakness, and they'll have no mercy. Our family history confirms that fact."

"I follow the voice I hear within me," Sebastian said. "What else would you have me do?"

"I tell you again: Give the cross to your brother if you are too morally weak to renounce the religion of the troubadours."

It was true what his father had said. These troubadours had no real sense of the God Almighty who guides our history and gives us a destiny. They were even lazier and more worthless than his brothers because their lives were at the beck and call, even at the command of the women they pretended, for the sake of an occasional favor in the dark (that, no doubt, was the truth of it) to worship; though not to worship in an authentically spiritual way as with the women who knelt at Sebastian's cross.

The troubadours worshipped his sisters in a pagan way, for the very fact of their flesh, of the breasts and hips they sang about, his sisters' and even sometimes his middle-aged aunts' buttocks, legs and feet, their hands and lips, their eyes, their voices, even for the way his sisters smelled. Their worship was effete, sickening, pathetically unconnected to the supernatural. They did not worship the divine spirit incarnate in his sisters. They worshipped the body itself.

That is what their songs of *amor* were about, even if they encircled the bodies they adored with poetic vaporings about flowers and stars. Body worship for its own sweet sake! Disgusting. He would have sent the whole band of troubadours packing if his sisters hadn't screamed that they would die of grief should their lovers be taken away.

Very well, let the women continue being titillated by their celibate concubines, just so they understood that he cared nothing any more for the gentler arts so gushingly spoken of at the dinner table by one or the other of those fellows he was forced to endure for the sake of his sisters and aunts. As if these fops were his own brothers, though in fact they had done what no brothers would do; they had seduced the souls of his sisters and stolen his right to their full attention.

While all those women out there in the world adored him, whatever his father said, because he gave them a vision of the sublime, his own sisters still considered him gross and even cruel in his understanding of a maiden's true desire. Let them.

His father had asked Sebastian one day more than a year ago, "If you continue to play the troubadour, do you know what they'll see? This crowd that comes to your crucifixion?"

Sebastian remembered how he had been practicing the steps to a pavanne at the time. He stopped, smiled at his father and asked indifferently, "What will they see?"

"They'll look up and they'll think they see a *woman* on the cross."

Sebastian burst out laughing.

Later, during his last and longest ordeal on the cross, he thought about his father's words and wondered what Abraham was thinking now, seeing his son take on twice the challenge of any other man in their family's history.

But Abraham was right. Sebastian saw it now. Divine love was the business of his family, not the profane love sung about in the romances. At the next tupping, he would be ready to do his duty without any thought for his own feelings, or for those of the bride. In fact, he would choose the girl who seemed to want him least. He would choose a bride who could remain like him, aloof from anything but the pure formality of sacred ritual.

The only true and worthy intention of their night beneath the altar would be the creation of a boy who would be the Christ. Then it would happen as God willed.

Yes, then it would finally happen.

SEVEN

AGAIN, WHEN THE PEACH TREES were in fragrant bloom, all the daughters of the serfs who wished to be married that spring lined up to be inspected by their Lord. Again he went out in his fine velvet robe to have a look at them. He walked up and down the line while they stood in their gowns of silver satin, the golden crosses each one had received as a gift from the Cristo-Reys glittering at their throats, their hair crowned with daisies, their feet humbly bare.

He checked them over carefully while the women and their brothers and his father in his big leather chair watched from the porch, his brothers from a balcony. Sebastian lifted each veil to study each face, no longer to see how gentle she might be, how docile or how soft, but how indifferent.

The young girl who cared for him least was standing last in line. He knew it the moment he inspected her, though he couldn't have said just why. A mysterious force held her in its sway, working on her spirit from afar. There was a shimmering from her wedding dress that sent a shudder up his spine. He took hold of her hand to steady himself, and was pleased at its iciness. There in the hot white sun of spring her wintry body, frozen at his touch, challenged and heated him.

He felt his ears burning as he finally lifted the veil and saw the pale, high-cheeked, strangely exotic face that let itself be looked at as if the girl inside were not in line among the brides at all. Her mind was far away. She might have been up some-where in the mountain all alone listening to a waterfall. There was no clue on her straight, full lipped, slightly pursed mouth, as to what she was feeling.

He wanted her. This was the bride that he must have even if

she only lay there like a corpse. Such surliness, so distant! He would make no effort to bring her back into his ken, to warm her, to force her to bring those faraway eyes back home. No. He and she were performers in a moral play. He would enter her as from a great distance, and from as great a distance she would receive him inside herself. Neither would be there in a worldly way. Yet between them their bodies would do what they must, and the mystery would flower without either one of them having made a sound.

Somehow he sensed that she wanted this just as ardently as he did. She did not want in the least to be possessed by him, but she wanted him to lie with her so that she could abandon herself in fantasy to the mystical body of Christ.

"Who is her father?" he asked.

From the group of men in straw hats under the chestnut tree, a short, thick shouldered peasant instantly stepped forth.

"Lord?"

He was a bull, this one. Sebastian remembered wrestling with him once. He remembered what a pleasure it had been finally to find a man among the peasants who was strong enough to throw him; how the man had seated himself on his chest in such a way that Sebastian could feel the power of the man's huge testicles.

It was up at the end of the valley where the finest beef cattle grazed, there on the grass not far from a herd of steers who had raised their heads from grazing to watch the men on horseback form a circle and lean forward in their saddles, chuckling along with Sebastian to see that, at last, they had a champion who could best the Cristo-Rey. Sebastian remembered how this fiery-eyed, bull-shouldered man had brought his knees together, clamping them against Sebastian's ribs, had seized Sebastian by the wrists and glared at the wounds of his stigmata as if he were angry to see them there. He'd gotten up, stood glowering over Sebastian, then stepped back, reached out, proffered his hand.

But then he'd pulled Sebastian to his feet with a grip so tight it shot lightning pain down into Sebastian's bowels, causing him to cross one knee comically over the other and shake his hand in the air. The men roared with laughter. Though he laughed with them, Sebastian blushed like a woman, and had to wipe the tears from his eyes.

The man had looked at his big hand as if he were ashamed of what it had done. He'd looked at the men in such a way as to quiet them down and to make them take their hands off the pommels of their saddles and to sit up straight, respectful in the sight of their Lord.

"Forgive me, Sire," he'd said.

Sebastian had regained his composure and managed to summon up fairly good spirits when he said, "Nothing to forgive, my good man. It was a pleasure to know who I can call upon when I need someone of strength."

Now, in front of the chapel, the man was again asking Sebastian to forgive him. Once more, Sebastian found himself saying, "Nothing to forgive, my good man."

But this time the answer was not, "Thank you, thank you, Sire."

This time, the man removed his hat. He wiped his brow, then set the hat back on his shaggy head, and slapped it down hard.

"I cannot give you my daughter. Bringing her here was a mistake. I only did so because she persuaded me—"

The man looked anxiously toward his daughter, as if asking for help. Sebastian, who had been holding her veil up all the while, looked into her eyes. She bowed her head so quickly that the veil tore from his fingers and dropped over her face.

He was thrilled. Of course. He saw it now. She had known he would choose her. She wanted so badly to be chosen that she had persuaded her father to bring her to the line of brides even though she had no plan to marry afterward. She was like a vestal virgin. This girl aspired, just as Sebastian did, to become a vehicle for divine possession, to remove all personal interest and to let her body be used only by a greater power. The mysterious intensity of their two presences so close together told him this.

Sebastian glanced at his chosen bride. Her face was hidden now. She was standing very straight, the veil draped over her upraised face.

Or is it . . .? A more troubling voice in Sebastian's head whispered to him. Is it that she simply desires me?

She was so unlike the daughter of a serf. So queenly.

Hadn't he learned from his brothers that women make themselves most desirable by holding themselves aloof? No, he scolded himself. He mustn't succumb to that. The father was giving Sebastian a daughter who desired nothing less than to become the bride of Christ.

Could Sebastian satisfy such a high spiritual ambition? He said almost gently to the girl's father: "Persuaded you of what?"

"I was a fool to believe it, Sire. She persuaded me that you would never choose the likes of her."

"Oh, but indeed, I have. Rest assured, I have never seen a virgin in this line whom I desired more. You thought a show of honest strength had lost you favor with the Cristo-Rey? Is that it?" Sebastian leaned back and bestowed a warm, generous smile upon the father of his bride.

"Well, have no fear. You'll see how much I prize a man who breeds a daughter such as you have brought me for the making of a son."

Sebastian took a firm grip on the girl, just below her shoulder where his fingers could push in under her arm. The arm itself was cool as marble, but the tips of his fingers found a hot, moist place that made him feel weak in the knees, he suddenly desired her so.

"What do you call this lovely girl of yours?"

"Sidelle, my Lord."

"Sidelle, indeed."

Sebastian was quite taken aback, for the name Sidelle had belonged to a pagan goddess whom the native people had worshipped before the conquest. Just as the Christian girls of that land would have their given name attached to the name of the Holy Virgin (Sebastian's sisters, for example, were named Maria Dolores, Maria Teresa, Maria Lourdes, etc.) so the name "Sidelle" had preceded the familiar names of the pagan women before the forced conversion to Christianity.

It struck Sebastian as some kind of marvellous portent that the father of the girl he had chosen as his bride had dared to give his daughter the name that belonged to the first of the subjugated women, the first woman to be bled, and to the goddess whose forests had also been ravaged.

Sebastian felt audacious when he looked at the girl as if he already owned her, and said her name in a frankly amorous way, "Maria Sidelle."

Her father strode to the other side of her and corrected him, saying, "It is simply Sidelle, my Lord."

Sidelle reached out and gave her father her hand.

"Well, then, we will have to give her a Christian name, and you a Christian title."

"I have no need of title or land, Sire. It is only because Sidelle wanted to be married that we risked coming here. Forgive us. It was a mistake."

"Quite so." Sebastian thought he would tease the man. "Whom would have your Sidelle marry, then?"

"She would marry one who would allow her to stay at home with me during his wanderings." He pulled at his daughter's hand. "I need her at home. Her mother has not been with us, you see."

Sebastian looked to the porch to see if his family was enjoying this scene.

"Why has her mother not been with her?"

"Because she is a healer, Sire. She lives alone in the forest, as healers must. I have only my daughter to care for me."

"Well then, hear this: Your daughter need not marry at all. After we have enjoyed her . . ." (When speaking of his sacred self, Sebastian sometimes found it difficult to refer to himself as 'I.') "she can return home to serve her father for the rest of his life, if that pleases her."

Sebastian let go of her arm and brought the hand that had held her to his chin. Feigning to rub his beard while thinking things over, he smelled her female heat upon his fingertips, breathed it down deep, sucking its vapors into the corners of his mouth. He dropped his hands to enjoy for an instant the arousal of his sex before he crossed his hands modestly in front.

"Unless . . ." Sebastian was astonished to hear himself say, "I choose to keep the girl with me."

It pleased him so much to see the consternation on the face of the bride's father that he could not resist adding, "Perhaps we shall even marry her," though he knew immediately by the flutter of gowns among the brides, and by the reaction of the people on the porch and balcony—the way they looked so shocked, especially his father half rising from his chair—that the jest was out of place.

Sebastian cleared his throat, placed his hand over his heart, and prepared to deliver the kind of flowery speech that was considered proper for the occasion:

"Bring us this child of yours tonight. You will be well rewarded. Bring us this bride and know that the Cristo-Rey gives out more than the usual boon to a man whom he admires not only for his prowess as a fighter, but even more for his prowess as a sower of fine seed. A full one hundred hectares of my finest land and grazing rights for your cattle throughout the high plateaux. Give me your daughter to be my Mary and you'll be rich and free."

The man said, "No. That cannot be. She has another destiny."

Sebastian drew back and stared at the girl's father in disbelief.

"She's promised," her father said.

"Yes? And what of that? All these girls are promised. That is why you brought them here, I presume."

"The one she is to marry . . ." The girl's father looked toward the porch of the hacienda. "He is not like us. He insists a girl be a virgin when she weds."

"In the eyes of God, she is as much a virgin as Mary was with Joseph."

The father smiled out of the side of his mouth. "I have said, she is not a Mary. With your permission, may I take her home now, Sire?"

Sebastian looked toward the porch where all seven of his sisters were seated across from each other in wicker couches, their faces turned sideways towards him. In the big chair by the door sat Abraham Cristo-Rey with the flock of his own sisters hovering around him. Some dozen gaily-dressed troubadours were seated along the railing, swinging their legs.

"You will bring her to us tonight," Sebastian proclaimed in a loud, stern voice.

"Forgive me," the father barked so loudly his voice echoed off the hills, "but Sidelle will stay where she must stay."

He released his daughter's hand, offered her his elbow, and walked off with her toward the orchard.

Sebastian was too taken aback to make a move. He stood there stock still while he watched the man lead the chosen bride calmly, with slow dignity away from that astonished line of girls who all were turned now, looking back through their veils, some of them even lifting the veils better to see what would happen next.

All watched the father lead her across the field and up into the orchard. The girl in the bridal gown and the peasant in his black pants, white tunic and straw hat disappeared between two tangled rows of grapevines.

 E I G H T

SEBASTIAN LET the other brides go home with their fathers. He hadn't the slightest desire to possess any except Sidelle. He walked back to the house past his silent family and the troubadours—let them think what they liked—and up to his room where he lay down on his bed with his hands behind his head.

He could not understand why he was feeling so secretly elated when he should have been enraged at the insult Sidelle's father had perpetrated upon him in front of everyone. He should have been thinking of just which way he would punish the man; in fact, he knew it was almost his duty to start doing so: whether to have him whipped or perhaps even to have him hung.

Yet Sebastian had to confess to himself that he admired the father of Sidelle for refusing to sell his daughter's blood for land and gold. This had never happened before. It took some reflection to realize that there was no law against it. Nobody had ever said that a virgin must surrender her body to the Cristo-Rey. The command was strictly formal, like commanding someone to accept a wonderful gift. The decision was never the girl's, of course, always the father's.

Sebastian thought about it long and hard, how he would not punish Sidelle's father; he would show the compassion of the Cristo-Rey. But he would have her nevertheless. He could visualize her face more clearly now than when he had actually seen it. A round moon face he would want to hold by the jaw, turn this way and that on its long, slim neck, and kiss on the pale brow, on the high, rosy cheeks, over the eyes, against each of those flared nostrils, hard on that soft, pushed out mouth of hers, brushing his lips then against her neck, turning her face to push her hair back with his nose and, breathing the fragrance of her heat, touch the tip of his tongue to the lobe of her ear. He would whisper her name.

God help me, he said to the one inside himself who was watching to see if he was cured yet of the infection called *amor*. I haven't escaped at all. I yearn for her.

"Sidelle," he said out loud, loving the sound of that name.

He said the name over and over, gazing at the angels that flew about the ceiling cupola. He imagined letting go of her jaw and hearing her fall back with a moan. He would undo her bodice, browse her body, press his hand firmly upon her knee.

One of the angels on the ceiling dome was playing a harp. This plump cherub had a mischievous, somewhat mocking look on his face. Sebastian could plainly hear him croak in an old dwarf's voice as he flew down close, "She'll struggle free just like that bride you tupped when you were young. The one you dragged down by the hair.

"You'll have to chase her," the angel croaked, "chase her and catch her and drag her to the altar." He affected one of those sickly sweet smiles that had always made Sebastian uncomfortable with the naked child-men when they came to life on his ceiling during his reveries.

"Unless you let her go," the angel whispered, and flew back to join the other winged cherubim and seraphim playing their instruments amidst the clouds. Together they sang, "Let her go, Cristo, let the girl fly to the boy she desires."

"No," he answered. "She's mine."

Who was it she desired so much that she could not allow her father to give her to another for the breaking of her hymen? An intense and thrilling emotion spread through his nerves and veins as he began to wonder about the man. Jealousy was such a new emotion to Sebastian that he could only recognize it as some kind of painful arousal.

It occurred to him that neither Sidelle nor her father might have been the ones to insist on her refusal. Maybe it was the boy himself? Maybe he had already committed the sacrilege of deflowering her before her womanhood had properly been sanctified.

Had some scoundrel who could have her for the rest of his life been so proprietary as to rob Sebastian of his one chance—and by divine right!—to taste and smell and touch and gaze upon her beauty, to hear that delicious cry that comes with the piercing. Could anyone be that selfish, to want the honey *and* the blood?

Sebastian jumped from his bed and ran to find the help he needed. He found Roman in the billiard room and told him to go find who it was this girl Sidelle so pined for that she could not grace the bed of the Cristo-Rey for one single night.

"Am I not her Lord? Very well, then, bring me the man she does call Lord and let me have words with him."

NINE

SEBASTIAN WANDERED down into the music room that afternoon, sat on the harp stool and pulled the harp towards him. Though he was awkward with the instrument, having reluctantly taken a few lessons only to please his sisters, he plucked at the strings and sang the words inside himself of how there is this force *amor* which he had tried to find, and then denied, and now would try again to summon from his soul. He didn't want to take Sidelle by force, he sang. He longed to have her love him in the way she loved the man her father spoke of.

As he was singing, into the room strolled the troubadour whose music these last years had brought such happiness to the people of the hacienda. Talifiero, the singer and harpist, having heard the rude twangs from Sebastian's harp had no doubt come to teach him how to pluck those strings more pleasantly.

Seeing the harpist over his shoulder, Sebastian acknowledged that what Talifiero had taught him he'd almost entirely forgotten.

Discreetly, Talifiero approached behind him, stretched forth his arms, and touched his finger tips to Sebastian's. He explained how his Lord must pluck the strings nimbly, with spirit and with full delight. Or, if there was a melancholy in his soul, then he must draw back like so, and strum more evenly, not lingering on this one string or that, but moving over all of them with fingers flowing like the breeze when it moans over the bending flowers. He reminded Sebastian how he must sing while he played, bringing the words up from his heart.

To this young troubadour, Sebastian sang of how he longed

to know a girl's love, a holy, pure and faithful love, to join his flesh to one who longed for him not just with her body but with her soul. He asked the Holy Virgin to send a girl as pure as She Herself was when God descended upon her. Sebastian vowed that he would lay that precious girl in a gentle place, up in a field, or even in a bed such as the bed of one who knows what wedlock is. He sang of how he longed for marriage to a lady old enough to know the ripeness of romance. Someone he could hold in his arms night after night, stroking her body, caressing her hair, his body tight against hers, his manhood sunk inside her womanhood all the night long.

And as he sang his heart out, Talifiero sang a harmony. He followed Sebastian into and out of every line. He helped find the words and sometimes rhymed them. He encouraged. He even gave the name Sidelle to the girl whose name Sebastian had not mentioned. He breathed across Sebastian's neck, letting him feel the heat of his own passion as they became four hands with a single throbbing heart for this Sidelle, their wild rose of the valley.

When he could sing no more, Sebastian laughed and fell back off the harpist's stool, his arms spread out with happy abandon. Talifiero lay aside his harp and came to sit beside his student. Sebastian could feel the backs of his hands throbbing where the nails were driven during his crucifixions.

They remained silent for a time, and then Sebastian sat up and looked at Talifiero, feeling a sudden huskiness in his throat.

"Thank you, my friend," he said. He got to his feet and started for the door.

"But, Lord?" the harpist called out, sitting up. "You haven't said why you sent for me."

"I didn't send for you. Remember? You heard me plucking at the harp and you came to the rescue."

"No. It was your brother who sought me out. He said that you had something to tell me."

"To tell you?"

Sebastian was so taken aback he could hardly speak. He swallowed hard. "Are you the one, then? That can't be. Why I—" He didn't want to say it. He had assumed that the man Sidelle loved was a person of exceptional manliness, not a mere *amator* of women. Sebastian was sure his rival would prove a match for his own manliness: one of the virile young peasants.

Talifiero hurried after him. They walked under the arches together while he told Sebastian in a voice that seemed suddenly girlish and really quite silly in tone, "Oh, yes, my Lord, I am the one who loves Sidelle. I am the man she would be faithful to. In the old country, I myself came from peasant stock, and so I looked for a bride among the families of the valley. And I found the perfect girl. I know you'll understand. You are a good man. How could someone who plays the Christ be other than a loving and forgiving man? She could not give herself to you," he said pleadingly. "Even her father, frightened as he is, knows he could never give his child to you because . . ."

"Because?"

Sebastian sat down on the stone railing, feeling so dizzy he almost fell back over the edge into the spire of a cypress tree. Talifiero put his hand on Sebastian's back to steady him. Sebastian shrugged him off, clenched his fists between his legs and looked at the harpist as threateningly as he could, considering that Talifiero remained so friendly and smiling.

"Oh, Sire," said Talifiero, "this is no time for such a look as that. Be happy for me. She loves me."

Sebastian brought his arm back. He struck the harpist's face so hard with the back of his hand that the old wound fired up and shot its pain deep down to his very toes. The sound of the blow had brought his brother Roman whom he told, right there in front of Talifiero, to go find the girl Sidelle and to bring her to the hacienda tonight.

"Tell her mother to dress her again in her bridal gown."

Sebastian felt strangely elated by a glimpse of blood running out from between the fingers of the hand that Talifiero held to his mouth. Talifiero was leaning against the wall between the pink arches under a tapestry of Abraham Cristo-Rey hanging on the family cross with all the women wringing their hands in prayer and supplication. It amused Sebastian to see the dainty harpist pull a jewelled dagger from his belt. Talifiero stammered a few ludicrous threats, embellished with leaps and starts. When he lunged, Sebastian had pity him, it was so easy just to seize him by the wrist and throw him down.

"Whether you jest or not," Sebastian growled, "take care." He bashed Talifiero, but not very hard, across the head with the side of his boot.

Talifiero lay there on the flagstones pretending to be unconscious from the blow, but obviously not, since tears were running down his cheek. Sebastian winked at his Aunt Maria Latona, who was standing in a doorway chewing on her knuckles.

"Tell me, Auntie. If we put him in a cage, do you think we can make him sing like the *hilgeuro*? Do you think he'll bring all the lovers down from the hills?"

"What I told you about the *hilguero* was a secret between us," she said, "Not to be spoken of in front of others."

"But look," Sebastian sneered. He's deaf to the world. Besides, he knows all about *Hilguero*, does he not? Isn't he one of those who drags you off to bed while the bird sings? Very well, let *me* do the singing now."

Maria Latona approached and reached a comforting hand toward Talifiero. But Sebastian seized her by the wrist and held her fast.

"Why do you look at him as if he was to be pitied?" Sebastian repeated a phrase that had been taught to him as part of the family catechism: "An insult to one Cristo-Rey is an insult to us all."

"How did he insult you then?"

"With an insult," Sebastian snapped. "Now, shall I call one

of the brothers to drag him to the dungeon? Or would you like to be the one who carries him there yourself? I'm sure you're quite strong enough, and willing. Yes, why don't you do it for me? Drag your pretty bird down to the cellar. And let him stay there until he finds himself inspired to compose a poem of apology for the insult I've just endured."

"Again I ask, what insult was that, nephew?" She hoisted the skinny Talifiero to his feet and brushed the dust from the poet's tunic.

As a matter of fact, Sebastian could not remember the exact gist of the offence, so he eased his wrath and said to the groggy harpist, "Be reasonable, good fellow. I'll have Sidelle only once. Perhaps she'll bear my child; but after that, just think, you'll have her for all of your life. You can father as many children as you please. While I . . . I'll go on somehow suffering my life away, never getting to be with her ever again. I'm the one who's to be pitied. You're the lucky one."

Talifiero spat in Sebastian's face.

IN THE OLD WINE CELLAR, there was one small barred window, no bigger than the window of a monkey's cage. At that window stood Sidelle's lover. While listening to him sing, Sebastian wondered: If Talifiero is as innocent and pure, as surely he must be to feel such ethereal love for Sidelle, what could he do to please her that I could not do even better, once she was in my arms?

If I were to be tender with her, to sing a poem or two, to touch her gently, to unlace her dress with slow consideration, surely she would love me just as sweetly as she loves him. Surely she would surrender willingly, even eagerly to me, once I was with her alone in the chapel in the candlelight.

Into the fantasy wove the voice of the singer in the prison. Uncanny that this lad, this gentle, beardless boy, hardly a man at all, imprisoned now, could sing such beauteous love songs about birds and flowers, could sing of walks by the river, and of trysts where nothing more was said than, Listen, hear, hear how the wind blows in the grass, my love. And she (Sebastian mused), she was swooning to the singer's feet, her arms around his legs, her adoring cheek pressed to Tailfiero's knee. Yes, hear him boast in his song of how he sank to his knees against her, how she took his head in her hands, kissed him on the brow and mouth and throat, how he rolled her over into the grass, opened the buttons down her back. The prisoner sang as if celebrating Sidelle with all the world.

Unseemly even that this lad could sing the phrases of his trystinqs with Sidelle when he knew that Sebastian could hear and that he would only be provoked into loving her even more ardently. For Sebastian was truly beginning to learn, or thought he was from listening to the songs of Talifiero, what love could be.

Disquieting to say the least that this boy could still so liltingly sing, as if with no concern, down there in his cage; that he could testify to all the world how soft her hand was, how wondrous her smile, how the glitter of her eyes appeared to his mind when sunlight glittered on a pool, how much her laughter meant to him when heard in the sound of falling leaves trembling down into the bottom of his heart.

Sebastian found the words too precious. Almost, he pitied such a girl as Sidelle to be enamoured of a boy whose songs showed such a lack of manliness. They were so flowery. He listened sometimes with disgust, listened and wondered, and even put his hands over his ears. He could never love quite that gushingly; he would be less talkative and more robust.

Yet he took his hands away again and listened more attentively than ever.

Perhaps he could.

He listened, haunted within himself by all that he expected, his body already aroused in anticipation of the night when he would be there with Sidelle in their stained glass house of God, the only house he'd ever known where he could sink his manhood into the lamb who gave her body, willingly or not, to God.

Why was Talifiero singing? Was it because he knew that Sebastian was listening? Was it to torment him? Why did he not scream in rage, or weep? Why did he flaunt his love hour after hour, chirping her name, Sidelle, Sidelle, Sidelle?

I too could love like that, Sebastian mused, though not perhaps with songs that seemed, like Talifiero's, to slip into the streams of air, blown from their cage off on the wind all the way to the farmhouse room where Sebastian's brothers, who had ridden to fetch her, must by now be telling her father in no uncertain terms that she would be bled on Sebastian Cristo-Rey's command whether she came to be bled with dignity or had to be dragged to the chapel by force.

Later Sebastian was to learn that they had not found her home. She had flown, her father said. He could not tell them where. Up into the hills somewhere. "Leave her alone," he'd said. "Sidelle's not for the likes of Sebastian Cristo-Rey. Tell him to find another girl. Or, better, not to take any girl at all away from a true communion with our Lord. Your lord's a blasphemer, an idolater, an outrage to the Christ whose role he plays. How dare he claim these girls for his own? They are not cattle to be branded. God put another less precious offering in Isaac's place. When will God provide a substitute for these our daughters? How long must we offer sacrifice like pagans? Go away."

As, with outraged countenance, Roman repeated the message Sidelle's father had sent to him, Sebastian could see that his other two brothers could not refrain from licking the taste of satisfaction from their lips.

Sebastian told them not to harm the father, but they confessed they already had. They'd beaten the insolent peasant, that was all. Knocked some sense into his head and let him go.

Sebastian said he could not blame them, really. Such impertinence.

"Sidelle? Did you find her?"

Roman looked curiously at his brother. Was it defiance? "We thought we should first ask Father whether we stand within the law to go out hunting for this reluctant bride of yours."

"What law?"

It had always seemed to Sebastian that the Cristo-Reys were deemed by the citizenry wise enough to abide only by the laws of their own making.

"Why, brother, the law of the land."

"Law of the land?" Sebastian was genuinely bewildered. "When have the laws of the outside world ever intruded on the valley of the Cristo-Rey?"

"Render unto Caesar," Roman warned.

Sebastian wanted to shout: Enough of that. Ride forth and find the girl.

But, so as not to seem impetuous or cruel when he meant merely to carry out his sacred duty, he said calmly, "Imagine how Sidelle and her family would feel when next they knelt before the cross if God looked down and saw a girl afraid to accept the seed of incarnation. Bring her to me for her own sake. Someone as beautiful as she should not have to carry the burden of guilt all her life for the mere hoarding of her maidenhead."

 ELEVEN

THEY FOUND SIDELLE up in the hills hiding in a tree. Sebastian's brothers climbed up and dragged her down. That is why, they explained after they had ridden up to the veranda and deposited her at the bottom of the stairs, he would find so many scratches on her arms and legs. That is why her head ran gouts of blood. She had been torn by all the thorny branches. It was not their fault. Gently as they had treated her, she had been in this condition when they hauled her down. And then they had remembered how Sebastian wanted her dressed as for a wedding with her God, so one of them had ridden back for the gown, and, when he'd returned with it, they had found it a nasty business getting her to take off her other dress and put this one on.

He had detested his brothers for the way they glanced at each other with twinkling eyes. Now, as she lay panting at Sebastian's feet, the wedding gown ripped and soiled, he perceived that she was listening to Talifiero. As soon as she heard the harpist's voice, she lay there, head raised from the dirt, listening as he poured out his song.

Sebastian thanked his brothers, sent them away.

When Sidelle and he were alone with no one watching, he knelt beside her. He reached under her perspiring waist. He lifted her up against his knee. She offered no resistance, but lay heavy upon his hand.

"My soft Sidelle. My mountain stream. My scent of roses on the air."

Other such phrases he babbled in imitation of the songs he'd heard. But nothing would stir her. He wondered if she even heard his voice. Exhausted and wounded as she was, she had her eyes wide open, alert. She was listening only to the singer in the cage.

Sebastian hoisted her up. He carried her across the courtyard to the chapel, down the aisle of the nave, up into the chancel where he sat her in the bishop's chair. He told her to compose herself; he only meant to take her for a bride this one night so that the Cristo-Reys might carry on their line.

"Surely you understand as well as I. Without . . ." He found this hard to say, for it seemed somehow ludicrous, even absurd, though it was his true belief, ". . . without the sacrifice of girls like you, the drama could not be played out. There would be no one born, as I was, to suffer the role of Christ. We are both instruments of God."

He turned his face away, thinking she might spit. But she lowered her eyes and stared at the fingers she was twisting in her lap.

"I am not the instrument of your God." Her voice was surprisingly clear and penetrating. "I belong to another."

"Don't you see?" he pleaded. "We have no choice. I only mean to do my duty. I'll take you for my bride just this one night. I'll love you if you'll let me. There are things I know about the ways of love. I learned them from your lover. Pretend I'm Talifiero, if you like. I'll do with you just as I know he does."

She smirked. She covered her ears with her hands.

"Dear girl, understand me. Only for this one night must you sacrifice. Is that so terrible? I've sacrificed too." He spoke to her as tenderly as he possibly could. "You'll see how gentle I can be."

He ventured to push her chin up with his thumb. He tried to make her look him in the eye. But she was listening to the one whose song penetrated the very stones of the chapel. She would not let go of his singing. Talifiero's high, wailing voice seemed to seep through every window, through the images of madonnas and saints, and to drift down from the tower, from the bells. The song rang off them in some invisible way, pouring the sound of his ardor into her body. Sebastian saw that she was transported, ghostly radiant, like a body with the spirit flown away.

"Compose yourself," he said, and dared to lay a hand hesitantly on one of her breasts.

She started. She slid back in the chair, rolling her eyes upward. In truth, he thought, she was not as beautiful as she might have been. Her pallor in the light of dusk through the blue and wine red windows made her look almost like a corpse. He took his hand away.

Again he said, "Compose yourself."

He could not bear to take this girl against her will. The prospect of another rape sickened him.

"I'll have one of my sisters bring you something to eat. At midnight I'll come visit you. There where you see that bed of straw, under the cross." He choked up, remembering the anguished drama of his annual play of sacrifice, suddenly sorry for himself and convinced that his crucifixion involved a much greater suffering than it ever actually did.

"That cross," he stammered, "which I have carried to Calvary ten times now, nailed to it longer than any man. Give me my due, Sidelle."

He swallowed so hard a pain blazed in his throat.

What a magnificent creature this girl was, for all her ghostliness. She brought her knees tight together as he knelt on the stone floor. With her bare foot, she tried to push him away. Such a slim leg, poignant with its dark scratches.

He pressed his forehead to her knee, closed his eyes, asked God to let him be for once a man who made a girl love, yes, truly love him as in the romantic songs. He promised that until she did he would not attempt to violate her.

Hearing Talifiero's distant voice grow ever more frantic, he said to himself, let her stay here and listen if it warms her flesh, if it excites her to be caged in here suffering his song.

Let her sit here in silence while he sings on. And when I do fire my seed into her body, let her womb clutch and hold it with all the passion she now feels for him.

Sebastian reached up and touched her hair. She turned her head. He opened his eyes, and took the hand away.

"You'll stay here in the chapel and wait for me, won't you?"

"You'll hunt me down if I do not," she said in that ringing disembodied voice he found so strangely commanding.

"I'll return only when you desire me to."

"You have me here to take against my will," spoke the voice from somewhere deep in the well of her long, lovely throat. And then the girl's throat choked up. She gasped, heaved up a dry sob, gave off a few faint, stifled shrieks.

But suddenly she was sitting up straight, glaring at him with wide-open eyes.

"If you want to love, give up this bleeding of the brides. Let the girls be virgins when we marry. I beg of you. Love us, Sebastian Cristo-Rey. I ask you in the name of your Jesus and your Mary and your Joseph. In the name of every family in this valley, show that you truly love us, as you say we are loved by the Christ. For your own Christ's sake, leave us alone."

"I am not like the others." He swallowed hard. "Believe me, I am not."

"Nor am I. I am someone you would be wise to send home now. My religion is not yours."

"I am not like the others," he repeated pleadingly.

"How are you not?" she asked in a pitying voice. "How else can you ever be? I warn you now, before you plant your seed in me your tree will die. Its leaves will fall. Its fruits will all dry up. I am of the *living* tree. Violate me, your cross is dead."

In the candlelight, her eyes seemed to catch fire. She opened her mouth wide. She gave off a hiss from deep in her throat. He had heard just such a hiss when he'd picked up a fallen nighthawk with a broken wing. The frightening sound filled the chapel, making the candle flames quiver.

She stretched her neck out. Her face moved close to his. "Sebastian Cristo-Rey," she rasped. "Impostor on the cross."

He left her there, and went to join his family at supper on the veranda, sending the best portions from their table to Sidelle that evening on a silver tray with a full flagon of the best red wine so that she might be more intoxicated, less self-possessed when next he visited her.

Later, when the meal was finished, brandy and coffee were brought out. They watched the setting sun from the veranda, the men and women of the Cristo-Rey. Looking off toward the hills above the vineyards, they listened to Talifiero's song. It was about a fish who swims upstream into a pool of golden light, about a leaf picked up and carried swirling in the wind over the mountain out of sight, about a blown out candle whose last wisp of white smoke flies off like a bird into the lover's soul to die with her.

The women began to weep loudly.

"When are you going to have a go then?" Roman asked, contemptuous of his sisters' tears.

The women quieted down to hear what Sebastian would say. "Have a go?"

"At the reluctant bride, Sebastian. And, for God's sake, give her a son before I have to go to the chapel and do the job myself."

So it had come to that? His brother could talk to him in this way, and he felt no impulse to strike out. He should send Roman packing, but instead he heard himself say in a weak voice, "Soon."

"Well, let us hope so," Roman grumbled. "I don't relish playing God. I'd rather play—"

"I know what you'd rather play. I'll have a go at her very soon, I've said."

The other brothers grunted their encouragement. They began to tell stories about the bastard boys they'd sired. Theories were offered on what it is that makes the male seed outrace a female to the womb.

Sebastian listened closely, taking another cigar and passing the box around. All the brothers of the Cristo-Rey lit up. Abraham, asleep in his chair, snored on. Details of seduction became explicit. The brothers bragged, glancing at their sisters mockingly as they compared their exploits.

The women said not a word, but watched the blood red streak of sunset on the ridge of the hills.

After it was dark, Sebastian sat there in a cloud of smoke, trying to ignore the ongoing song of Talifiero, which could be heard ever more weakly now from the dungeon around the side of the house.

He noticed that the troubadours were coming to the steps one at a time to invite this or that sister or aunt out into the darkness for a stroll. Long after all the women were gone, Abraham awoke and clapped his hands for one of the women to bring more brandy. But none were within earshot. Nor did any of the servants seem to be around.

The singing from the dungeon faded away . . . and stopped.

Sebastian listened to the silence with alarm. He pushed back his chair, slapped his hands on his stomach.

"Well, then, brothers, the time has come."

The brothers shouted a lusty cheer as Sebastian set forth for the chapel, taking long, decisive strides.

But he never got that far.

 T W E L V E

AN IMPULSE STOPPED Sebastian at the corner of the house. The dim candlelight flickering red and blue through the windows of the chapel threw just enough light so that he could find his way to the door he sought.

The latch was fastened from outside with a bolt. He grabbed it with both hands, slammed it aside, and pulled open the door.

He felt his way down earth-encrusted steps into the cellar.

The sour air smelled of what? . . . The poet's piss.

"Harpist, where are you?"

No answer.

"Talifiero, listen."

Sebastian's breath came short and hoarse, as if he had run a great distance. "I've contrived a plan that should make us both happy. Are you listening?"

Sebastian could hear the thrum of the insects outside, the distant wail of a night animal up in the hills. He took a deep breath, composed himself.

"Hear me, Talifiero. If I were to let you go to Sidelle, would you still let me claim the child as my own?" He turned to speak in another direction. "Would you? If she conceived?"

Sebastian's voice echoed off the stone walls. "Are you there?"

The cellar was pitch black. Sebastian held his breath, listening for Talifiero's breathing.

Not a sound.

"Don't play *Hilguero*. You're not a bird, and you're not dead. I know that you're down here quite alive."

The threatening sound of his own voice frightened

Sebastian. He spoke more coaxingly. "Men don't die from singing their hearts out. If they did, I myself would have died a long time ago. Listen to me, good harpist. What if I let you go to her in my place? Could you return the favor? Could you leave her after your night of love? I shall stay down here and pray that you conceive a boy child. It would be my salvation, you know. I would be forever grateful."

Had he heard a faint sound of someone scoffing him? No, he'd imagined it. Sebastian cleared his throat, and spoke more earnestly.

"I'm used to long hours in a deathly place like this. If you know how to sing when you're down in this tomb, believe me, I know how to pray. I'm sorry I made my poor aunt drag you here. I'm sure she apologized a thousand times. My word is law with the women of our house, so you'll have to forgive her. Your anger should be turned entirely toward me. But, it would be better still if you understood and forgave me."

Sebastian could not control the almost whimpering tone in his voice: "I only wanted you to know something of what I feel, always alone, on the other side of life from other men, longing for the women who are there beyond the stone. Every year they lay me in the tomb, from Good Friday to Easter morning. After the women anoint me and wrap me in a winding sheet, the soldiers carry me down, leave me there, they roll the stone against the entryway. Oh, then, my friend, Sebastian Cristo-Rey has to do some fancy twisting to set himself free."

Sebastian suspected now that he was speaking to a corpse. But he talked on.

"I'll stay down here just as I do when I'm in the tomb. I'll pray for you. I'll pray for you and your Sidelle as if I really were the saviour of the world carrying you and our common bride through the dark night to a brighter shore."

Sebastian was moved almost to tears by the poetry his voice had found. He remembered Easter mornings when the stone was rolled back; what joy overwhelmed him as he breathed in the fresh air, stepped out in his winding sheets, appeared to the three Marys, then made himself vanish behind a screen set up for the occasion. What elation to hear the angel standing nearby cry out! To hear that child's voice proclaim to the great number of the devout who had gathered to witness the occasion: *Do not be afraid. You are looking for Jesus of Nazareth who was crucified. He is risen; he is not here.*

It had always made Sebastian feel bitter that he did not have a son to play this role, for he had played the angel at his own father's resurrection from the time he was old enough to remember the lines until he was too much a grown man to speak them angelically.

For some reason he could not control, he felt compelled to speak with the same tone he had used so many years ago when he was that angel-boy of the annunciation, even though now he was saying very different words at a very different occasion, and to someone he was quite certain now, with a growing dread, that he had caused to die of a broken heart.

"After you're through with her, have her wait for me in the chapel. Return to your quarters. Do not be afraid. In the morning, just before dawn, I shall go to the altar where she lies. I shall bring her to my house. To all the world, it will be as if not you, but she and I, had lain together. Do you hear me? What of that?"

Sebastian held his breath and listened.

It seemed to him that he could hear a faint breathing over to his right, near where the window was. Reaching out his hands so that he would not strike his face against a barrel or a post, he took a few wary steps in that direction, and stopped.

"Think. If she conceives a Christ, nobody will know but the three of us. That will be our secret spiritual bond for all time. Then, after she gives birth to the holy child, you must promise me to leave with her. Leave this village. Leave the country. I'll make it worth your while. Go now. Make love with your Sidelle. Engender me the son. Then each of us will have our dream. Do you hear me? You'll have Sidelle and I'll play this role of Christ until a ripe old age."

Sebastian held his breath again.

He could no longer hear the breathing?

"Talifiero?"

A sound of the breeze from outside moaned a vague harmony against something metallic. He turned to see the pale glow of the little barred window now. He groped his way toward it along the wall.

"Do you hear me, harpist? Go fly to your mate. You're free."

Sebastian bent down, brushing the air with his hands.

"See how I trust you? You could stick your dagger in my throat. But you'll forgive your poor unloved Christ of the Cristo-Reys. You'll forgive me, won't you, Talifiero? And you'll hasten to the chapel for my sake? You'll love her with true *amor.* On my honor, if you'll do that, not just for me but for the Christians of this land who need a son from me, I'll pay you all you need so that you can fly somewhere far, far away, you and your beautiful Sidelle. I'll put enough gold in your purse so that you can stop your wandering and put down roots, build you a home, plant and reap and sit in the sun singing, with as many children around you as the two of you desire. Give me a son and I'll give you the kind of marriage I myself could never hope to know except in dreams."

Sebastian turned in all directions, feeling about.

He fell to his knees in the dirt, reached out, reached up. But his arms and hands could only tangle with the spider webs. He could see a star now through the little window.

"Are you alive?"

He heard the panic in his voice echo against the dungeon walls.

"Harpist, forgive me."

Sebastian felt someone brush past him. He heard two quick, light footsteps on the stairs, and Talifiero was gone.

Sebastian sat down under the window in the dirt. He leaned back against the wall.

THIRTEEN

I AM the shadow of Christ.

I am this darkness.

What are these wounds in my hands but the wounds of the sorrowing women? I belong in the tomb forever. If I were truly brave, as I pretend to be while carrying the cross, I would put an end to all this once and for all. I would marry.

Out there in the chapel is the man I would have liked to be.

I have pulled open the door of the chapel.

Sidelle?

She sees me in the candlelight. Down the aisle I race. I race down the nave to the altar. She throws open her arms.

She opens her body.

I have entered her. She has entered my soul. We are one flesh.

Sebastian Cristo-Rey drew up his legs, and wrapped his arms around them. He pressed his forehead hard against his knees until a circle of pulsing yellow light opened in his forehead.

In that circle, he saw himself by candlelight lying under the altar with Sidelle. His body was stretched stiff and eager from toes to neck as he rested his weight on his hands, and raised up between her spread legs. He placed his rod just there where she was soft and open. With one hard thrust he drove it in.

Ahhhh.

He looked down at her with a fierce pride, his teeth clenched. Her dress was up around her waist. Her breasts were bare. He lowered his head and took one of her swollen nipples into his mouth. He was moving slowly in and out of her while she clutched at his buttocks.

Yessss, she was saying.

Sebastian let go of his knees; he opened his eyes wide. In the corner, darker than the blackness, he saw the hulks of two old barrels, like ancient animals watching him. These were the barrels that had stored the sacramental wine during those first years his ancestors had come to the valley.

The old ancestors watching.

He slid down the wall until he was stretched out on his back on the soft earth, only his head against the stone.

Sebastian, my love. Yes, yes, my Lord and love.

The Cristo-Rey spread his arms, spread his hands wide, his fingers stretched out. He closed his eyes, and saw himself being carried by his brothers to the cross. They were dressed as centurions. They laid him down carefully so that the edges of his buttocks and the base of his spine were resting on the little sitting bar. He crossed his feet the way he wanted them, with only his left foot on the platform, and felt the cords being wrapped around his ankles, the knot cinched tight, the cold spike being slipped between his two feet, then driven into place. Now he could feel the way Roman held him by the wrists and placed his, Sebastian's, hands over the notches where the spikes were to be driven. He felt the greased spikes being pushed into his hands, the almost pleasantly painful spreading of the bones and tendons.

Then it seemed to Sebastian that he could actually hear the spikes being driven into the wood; the ring of iron against steel.

Listen!

Was it true? Was it true, then, what he'd heard in the songs of the troubadours? That a woman could shriek with pleasure like that? Not with grief or with pain, but with a sound beyond dying. With such ecstasy?

Yes, he could hear her. Sidelle. Her mouth wide open, like the mouth of a singing angel crying out with gladness.

O! O!

He drove his body into hers.

Ah!

Yes!

He shot his heat into her, his fire. He felt it ignite her womb. Her womb swelled to radiance, like a sun. Her belly rose and fell. She lay very still.

Down from the little window, a cool breeze whirled. A new life streamed into the white light of her womb.

She let loose a howl that was heard in the hills until animals and birds answered back with their crooning.

His back arched up.

He sank down, utterly content.

Sebastian slept.

F O U R T E E N

SEBASTIAN AWOKE while it was still dark outside. He stood and stretched and looked up through the barred window at the stars. He must not have slept as long as he thought, but he felt entirely rested. It was too early to go find Sidelle in the chapel. Talifiero would still be with her. According to the songs, truly amorous lovers make love again and again, and are slow to arrive at the actual sowing of their seed.

So he had heard, so the songs went. He would go sit on the veranda and wait until he saw Talifiero come into the house.

Sebastian groped his way to the cellar stairs. The door was open. The fresh breeze smelled delicious. He spread out his arms, and looked up at the stars. They had never shone so brightly. I am a new man, he told himself. I am not who I was.

The path in front of the veranda pulsed with a pale white glow.

His body felt so light that it seemed to him his feet scarcely touched the ground. After he had climbed the stairs to the veranda, he sat himself down in his father's chair, and gave over to pleasant speculation on how he would raise his son. So appropriate did it seem that the images he conjured up be accompanied by the playing of a harp that it was some time before Sebastian came to his senses and realized that, indeed, he could very faintly hear harp music somewhere inside the house. He lit the oil lamp on the table and carried it through the grand salon and out into the patio. Around the far side of the patio were the guest quarters. He entered a corridor, pursuing the sound of the music until he found it farther back in a second small patio that had sometimes served as a cloister.

Talifiero was seated under a lemon tree playing the harp.

"What?" said Sebastian. "You've left her so soon?"

The music stopped. Sebastian approached.

"Yes, thank you, my Lord."

Sebastian sat down on the edge of a circular fountain, placing the lamp beside him. In the flutter of light and shadow, Talifiero, looking up, appeared to be distraught.

"And you did lie with her?"

"I fornicated under your command, Señor."

"She must have been very happy that it was you, not I, who came to her."

"Happy? Yes, Señor. Too happy, I think, for we were so quickly in each others arms and swept away by passion that it was over almost before it began. I confess to you, I was afraid you would change your mind and come running to take my place."

The harpist chuckled bitterly.

"But I didn't."

"So considerate of you, my good Lord. No, you did not."

"There will be other times for loving her without panic or fear."

"When will that be, Sire?"

"After our child is born."

"*Our* child?"

"Yours. Mine. Hers. Did you explain to her? Was she pleased? Did she think that was fair?"

There was a long silence. Someone in a room off the patio muttered in his sleep. Sebastian felt a moment of panic, but let it pass.

Finally, Talifiero said, "Yes. Yes, while we were lying there under your cross, I did try to explain. I told her that she must pretend she had been bled by you. And, if she conceived a child, to let the child be yours. And . . ."

Talifiero played a swooning sound over the harp strings.

"And what? What did she say?"

"Nothing, my Lord. That is when she fell into a faint. I thought she must have died, she lay so still. Yes, for a long time I was sure that it was just as I had known while I was down there in your dungeon singing, as your sisters say, like the bird *Hilguero*, singing my heart out, until I knew that she had sent her soul to heaven rather than lie with you. And I, too, was lying there in the prison almost dead, waiting for God to mercifully take my spirit away."

"But you were not in the prison now, and she was not dead."

"Not dead. Oh, no, *seigneur*. I knew she was not when I finally thought to place my ear to her breast. God be praised, I heard her heart still faintly beating."

"And what did you do then? A kerchief dipped in cool water from the font?"

"Oh, no, Señor. That is holy water. I would not have dared. Another remedy came to mind."

Sebastian saw Talifiero's eyes brim with tears.

The harpist smiled sadly. "Talk of water brings water to my eyes." He dried his eyes on the ruff of his sleeve, lay the flats of his hands across the harp strings, and plucked one single note so full of some strange pain that a lemon fell from a tree shadowing the fountain, and splashed into it, warping Sebastian's reflection as he looked down at himself. He watched himself dissolve.

"But you revived her?"

"Sire, I remembered what I'd heard: how brandy can revive a faint? And so I left her there in the straw at the altar, and I ran out of the chapel to the house. Up to the veranda I ran. The brandy bottle was there on the table. I filled a glass and I hurried back, holding my hand over it so that it wouldn't spill. But then, my Lord, at the door of the chapel, such an apparition that I was stopped in my tracks. The glass of brandy fell from my hands. It was so dark, I didn't know what had loomed up before me. And then I thought, here comes a wise man from the East, and I fell to my knees. See? Here? Can you see this bloodied knee? The brandy glass had broken. I was kneeling on the shards."

"What is this babble?" Sebastian demanded to know. "So then, you're just telling me a story, are you, harpist?"

"Sire, no. I saw a wise man. Or I thought I did."

"Are troubadours nothing but singers and tellers of lies? I want the truth now, nothing more."

"I'll hang myself before morning if what I say is false."

Sebastian looked up to the stars in supplication. "You're telling me you saw a wise man at the door of the chapel? Is that it?"

"A man on horseback was there blocking my way. I was frightened, not knowing who it was. I thought he might be Melchior, or Balthazar, or . . . what's the other one . . . because he wore a turban. But then he dismounted, and I knew."

"You knew what?"

"I am trying to tell you, Señor. The wise man was her father, you see. His head was bandaged. He was in a bad way. Very angry too. He said that his daughter would not be raped by the Cristo-Rey. He had come to take her home if it was not too late, and neither you nor any of the Cristo-Reys would stop him."

"Yes? And did you tell this ghost of her father that it was too late?"

"Exactly, Sire. I said to him that you had already bled her and that he had best ride on home because there was nothing any of us could do about that now. You had gone to bed already, I said, and sent me to bring her back to the house of the Cristo-Reys once she regained her wits."

"And so? What did her father do then?"

He told me to go back to my own bed. That he would take Sidelle home in any case. He was not kind with me, Señor. He said that none of this would have come to pass if she had chosen to remain unmarried all her life. He said that if I had not courted her, she might have remained at home, safe from the

Cristo-Rey, but that I had made her love me in a hopeless way. Hopeless and helpless I had made her, that is what he said. It was my fault, he said. I was the one who convinced her you would not tup her, and that if you did you would never lie with her against her will."

Talifiero dropped his hands from the harp. "Truly I did think so, my Lord. And now, see what you have done?"

"But I have done nothing," Sebastian said.

"No, my Lord. I mean, that is what her father said to me. He dismounted, tied up his horse, and he pushed me aside. 'See what you have done, you foolish boy,' he said. 'Now the false Christ,' these were his words, Señor, not mine, 'the false Christ has tupped her. He has ruined my daughter in the eyes of God and men. She is neither good for you nor anyone else,' he said. And I said, 'No, no, I love her still. I would take her gladly as she is. If she conceives a child from the Cristo-Rey, let him have the child, and then I'll marry her, you can be sure.'

"I said all this, Señor, and all he said to me was, 'Get back to your bed, lad, before I lay you low. Neither you nor anyone else will have my daughter now.' And so I came back here to play my harp and pray."

"Pray for what, harpist?"

"Pray that when you send out your men to bring her back again, you won't be too cruel."

"I won't send my men out," Sebastian said. "She'll stay at home until her father brings her to our chapel to be married on your wedding day. Tomorrow you will go tell him it was you who deflowered the bride. You'll tell him that the wedding should take place as soon as possible."

Sebastian turned back to the harpist. "Next year, I'll go out courting, just as you have. And when I've found a girl who loves me, I'll marry her. What do you think of that? I'll have my child in the normal way, and you'll have yours."

"Oh, splendid, my Lord. Splendid. God be praised for

opening your heart."

Talifiero leapt from his harp stool. He seized Sebastian's hand, and bent to kiss it.

When the singer's lips touched his wound, Sebastian felt a delicious tingling all along the ridges of his scar.

 FIFTEEN

IT WAS THE CUSTOM among the men and women of the Cristo-Rey every morning at the break of dawn to rise, put on their robes, enjoy coffee and sweet rolls together in the dining room while a few of the older women were out taking the covers off the bird cages, and then, when the birds were pleasantly singing, to walk in processional fashion from the grand salon out along the veranda under the portico and across the yard between two rows of cypresses down a gravel path to the chapel, there to kneel in prayer before the family cross.

Later, any house guests were welcome to enter the chapel and pray with the Cristo-Reys, but not so early as to interrupt that special intimacy the family shared in the presence of the venerable cross, blackened with age, upon which according to family legend, more than one hundred generations of Cristo-Reys had allowed themselves to be nailed since first the cross was fashioned (by the brother of a certain famous carpenter, so they liked to believe) for the enactment of their sacred profession.

In truth, the cross was not really so much a Christian symbol to the Cristo-Reys as it was a symbol of their family's peculiar vocation. The men and women of the Cristo-Rey did not kneel each morning in gratitude to God for the many blessings of wealth and honor that had come their way. They knelt more in gratitude to their ancestors.

The first light of dawn was still dim on the horizon when they entered the darkness of the chapel. The rays of the sun had not yet touched the windows. The red votive candles that usually flickered around the little doll bride in her glass case had all been blown out. Each family member glanced at her, as he or she always did, while they dipped their fingers in the font and crossed themselves. The glow of her dress could be seen in the dark, but her face and arms and legs were still lost in the bed of purple velvet on which she lay waiting for God.

Abraham, having learned that Sebastian had disgraced the family tradition by sending Sidelle home with her father without having lain with her, was in a dismal mood. He did not even cross himself. He sat down on the farthest pew back, his knees too shaky for kneeling. He rested his arms on the pew in front, dropping his forehead onto the folds of his robe.

The women had seated themselves in the pews to the left near the center of the nave, close together so as to be able to whisper to right and left and over their shoulders. They should have been silent, surrendering themselves to God in prayer, looking up at the family cross which, except during Holy Week, had hung above the altar so many hundreds of years. But they were loath to raise their eyes. They should have been venerating their ancestors through the spirit of that cross upon which so many generations of Cristo-Reys had been nailed, but this morning they were not so inclined.

There had been something of an orgy that night up in the orchard with the troubadours, at least as much of an orgy as men and women sworn to chastity can enjoy. Each of the women, in her own breast, was suffering from it now, wondering what had aroused her to such lustful abandon at the very same time that Talifiero, their *hilguero*, their wonderful singing bird was, for all they knew then, dying of grief in the dungeon of the hacienda, while Sebastian, in the chapel, raped the girl whom their dear harpist loved.

If Sidelle were indeed the mate to their *hilguero*, as Maria Latona, their most reliable gossip, insisted she was, perhaps the dear child might even have died from the bleeding. What then? It seemed as if, in some weird way, they had enjoyed themselves at the expense of Talifiero and Sidelle.

Wondering about this, some of the women were embarrassed at how voracious they had been. In fact, there was some confusion in their minds about whether they had actually remained chaste, whether the way they and their lovers had learned to arouse one another without actually consummating the act of cohabitation had left them exactly intact as virgins. Nevertheless, their wombs at least remained inviolate, and their flesh was tingling with a marvelous contentment such as they had never felt after other nights when they grew impatient and, silencing their lovers' poetry and song, let them touch them, stroke them, let their hands tease them under their clothes.

Last night had been different. Oh, their eyes said as they glanced at one another, what a secret we have!

They were more thrilled than ever to have found men whom they now knew possessed the magical dexterity not only to tease a woman to the edge of bliss, and then to leave her there so that she might carry her passion up to God, but knew how to force her passion over the edge and down, down, into the abyss of worldly happiness. Were there any other men on earth except these troubadours who knew the subtle and deliciously maddening secrets of pleasing a woman's flesh without actually breaking her hymen?

The Sisters of the Cristo-Rey were all convinced that, by some stroke of luck, or by the grace of God, or by their brother's marvelous forbearance, they had become intimate with a kind of love no other women in the world could even imagine.

Such was their provincialism.

Each one wondered whether the other women had been as lucky as she in finally discovering the gift their own lover had given her last night up there in the orchard under the stars: the journey past that excruciating peak, up, up, and finally over to the other side . . . the flowing downward, the warm, pleasing descent of passion that comes to rest in quiet joy.

Yes, surely.

Surely their troubadours had conspired to take all of them that night to the end of the journey, though the men themselves had held back. Next time, the Sisters of the Cristo-Rey told themselves, they would do likewise for the man who loved them. They would see to it that he too passed beyond the brink. They would enjoy the sound of his own stifled cries, as he had laughed so delightedly on hearing theirs. Reminiscing, the women of the Cristo-Rey were too ashamed to look up at the family cross. Too ashamed and too happy. Maria Latona was especially shy of looking at the cross, exhilarated as she was by her remorse. Last night, she had finally gone too far.

She had always known she would do so some day. She had disgraced the Sisters with someone; she wasn't sure which one he was. According to the way she told it later to Sebastian, when she tried to explain her pregnancy, she had been lying there, listening to the hard breathing and murmuring and squealing of the others, teasing the man beside her with her fingers, as she had been taught to do, when the scoundrel (she was glad she didn't know which one he was) crawled on top of her and, before she quite realized what was happening down there, he had pushed it inside of her, this tool of his which she had so solidly aroused. She had felt the hot discharge of his seed, his sudden softness, his quick withdrawal. It had been horrible and wonderful at once. What if a child had taken root inside her womb? The thought sent a warm flush of blood through her whole body, then made her shiver with sudden cold. She would be cast out. She had heard stories of other sisters in former times who had disgraced the Cristo-Rey. They'd vanished and were never heard from again.

This is my punishment, Maria Latona thought, for doing my brother's bidding, taking our sweet songbird down to his dark, cold cage. But, with that thought, she had to suppress a strange thrill that sent little bursts of fire through her nerves and veins.

She wondered: Did I take some kind of pleasure in putting

dear Talifiero into the dungeon?

No, she had done it from instinct, from an old training to duty. She had joined in the humiliation of the harpist out of that blind and foolish obedience the women of the Cristo-Reys felt they owed to the senior among their men. But if she hadn't put Talifiero in prison Sebastian would have called one of his brothers to do it, and wouldn't that have been much worse? They would have given him a few kicks before throwing him down the cellar stairs. At least, she told herself, I put him in his prison in a very kindly way. God could not punish me for that.

Indeed, she had taken Talifiero to the cellar by way of the kitchen, where she'd stuffed his pockets with bread and cheese, and stuck a wineskin under his arm. While she conducted him to the cellar, she laid her own shawl over his shoulders, and she kissed him good night at the door before she asked his forgiveness. Receiving it, she had shut the big, heavy cellar door, and bolted him in.

Maria Latona remembered how all the women and all their lovers had sat in the grass under the peach trees listening to the harpist sing. It was so dark, she did not even know whose lap she had lain her head in, whose hand had been stroking her hair. That wispy voice sent out through the window of the dungeon seemed to hover above the trees, and spread its sound out thinly on the air, like angel-song.

When the singing stopped, it seemed the wind had stopped blowing. Not a sound could be heard anywhere across the landscape. For some moments, nobody stirred, and then a hand slipped up under her long skirt. The hand squeezed hard, kneading at her thigh. She heard the stirrings around her, the groans of the other women, the doglike panting of the men. The earth began to shake. For all she knew, all of her sisters, all of her nieces had also lost their virginity last night. What would they all do then?

Her most secret parts were pleasantly sore. Even deep inside, despite herself, she continued to feel deliciously aroused, wondering what it would be like to have a house full of mothers with their children. She had a vision of herself lying back in an easy chair in the salon with an infant at her breast, and in the chairs and sofas all around other bare breasted women giving suck.

With such visions as these, Maria Latona hadn't the nerve to lift her eyes to the cross, as she told him later when she, of all the women in the house, had become the only one to talk with him, to tell him anything. She had been too busy trying to understand her own guilt, to comprehend the horror up there. When she did look up, she thought she was seeing a vision of her own punishment, a mere imagining.

Yes, a feeling of bad faith kept every one of the Cristo-Reys, not just the women, from wanting to look up with their usual expressions of pious wonder at that somewhat intimidating black cross.

The brothers were still stunned and amazed by the news Sebastian had given them that morning, that he would never again command one of the virgins to play the role of Mary to his God; that next year he would be wed to any maiden in the valley who would have him and that, as far as he was concerned, his brothers were free to marry any time they wished, let Father rant and rave if he must.

If the brothers had looked at their cross, it might have accused them of being too delighted with all this news, or too dismayed, depending on the wild swings of mood they were undergoing.

Each had sat down in a pew to the right of the aisle, making as much space between himself and the others as possible, wanting to ponder the full import of Sebastian's pronouncements.

Each of the brothers was now on his knees, hands clasped at his forehead, pretending to pray while he remembered this woman and that, wondering, with mixed happiness and dread, what it would be like to take her as a wife.

Memories of wenching were easily aroused for the brothers by the smell of the hay that was still strewn up there at the altar as bed for the bride who, they were mortified to think, had never been properly laid there, nor seigneurially bled.

Sebastian was the only one among them whose eyes had been fixed upon the cross. He had been the first to enter the chapel. As was his custom, he had walked straight down the aisle to kneel on the velvet cushion that was always there for the Christ of the family, at the foot of the chancel stairs between the two aisles.

Sebastian was kneeling with shoulders squared, back erect, hands together at his breast, mouth wide open, very stiff and still, like someone turned to stone. He had not moved in the least since first raising his eyes to the cross. He had opened his mouth and tried to scream. His mouth was still agape, but no sound had yet issued forth.

She had seemed like a ghost to him at first. An apparition in pale, smoky white. Like one of those traditional plaster saints that drip with blood and tears.

As his eyes adjusted to the dark, he grew more and more appalled by the realization that he could not make her stay that way. She was turning into a substantial creature of actual flesh and blood before his eyes, though mostly drained of blood except for the thick flow that dripped upon the altar from the edges of her hands.

Sebastian saw it clearly now, even to the wisps of hair across one eye.

Sidelle was up there.

The bride Sidelle, in her wedding dress, was nailed to his cross.

SIXTEEN

HER TOES BARELY TOUCHED the little platform.
Her feet were crossed. Her ankles were tied with a rope to the
mast. One knee was crossed over the other. Her head was
tilted to one side, almost resting on her shoulder. Her eyes
were open, rolled back, unblinking.

His eyes glazed over. He could no longer see the blood,
though he could hear it drip.

She kept changing in his blurred sight into a fish, a rabbit, a
white snake, a flow of yellow light. She became himself. He
saw somehow that he and she were the same person up there.
He was looking down upon himself, seeing himself as a
woman in mourning, dressed in black. He would have wailed
loudly, howled his grief, but not a sound would issue from his
throat.

And now Sidelle was up there again for a moment before she
turned into a white stag, and then a ghostly mass of hair.

He tried once more to release the scream stuck deep in his
throat. It pushed to get out, choked him. When it finally broke
forth, he realized that all the women were screaming with
him. Their horror echoed off the arches and the domes until
everyone was silenced at once by a great bellow from their father.

"Get her down from there!"

The brothers rushed past Sebastian; they scrambled up onto
the altar. They lifted the cross down, and still Sebastian could
not move. It seemed to him that he was kneeling now far from
all this, in some distant place, in a garden somewhere, alone,
behind a rock.

But his father was suddenly behind him, hands thrust under Sebastian's arms. He pulled Sebastian to his feet, threw him aside, and let him stumble against a pillar where Sebastian took hold, pressed his cheek against the cold marble, shut his eyes, and held on tight.

"Pull out the spikes!" commanded Abraham.

When Sebastian finally let go, turned and looked toward the chancel, he saw that his brothers had laid the cross down on the straw. They were crouched around Sidelle's body, busy at work. Sebastian could only see her feet being untied.

He looked back and saw the women fleeing.

Something made him glance up into the choir loft. He thought he saw Talifiero up there in the shadow, leaning against the wall beside the organ. Sebastian closed his eyes an instant, looked again. The harpist was not there. Quickly he looked back to Sidelle.

"Is she dead?" asked Abraham.

Roman held up the two bloody spikes, which he had re-moved from the hands. Four of the brothers lifted her limp body from the cross. Abraham approached, as did Sebastian, close enough so that he could see her now.

Abraham bent down, pressed his ear to her breast.

The brothers holding her remained very still.

The first rays of sunlight struck the east windows. A shaft of stained light shone at an angle across Sidelle's body, reflecting red and blue glints off the white gown.

Sebastian saw that her face was very pale, her mouth flaccid, her tongue protruding over her lower lip.

Abraham Cristo-Rey raised his head. He looked at his sons sternly. "We'll keep her here on the straw until our business is done."

Sebastian found his voice, "Is she dead then?"

"You'll watch over her while I ride to the lodge for the medi-cines. The rest of you know what has to be done. Her father will not be an easy man to kill. Before you go after him, the women must be silenced, shut away until the troubadours are sent packing. See to it that they leave at once, and make sure they'll never want to come back. No one must ever know our cross was violated in this way."

"But is she dead, father?"

"She is still alive."

SEVENTEEN

THEY THOUGHT they would lose her. She was unconscious for three days and nights. On the fourth day, there was a terrible pounding on the chapel door. The noise and its reverberations awakened her. She opened her eyes.

But when the pounding and the shouting stopped her eyelids fluttered and fell. She was gone far away again.

While Abraham administered his balms, Sebastian knelt close to her in the straw. He placed the tips of his fingers on her neck. Her heartbeat was faint and irregular. She did not appear to be breathing at all through her wide-open mouth.

The cross still lay on the floor. He looked at it, and shuddered.

If she should die, how could he go to the cross ever again? She would be up there with him. He would feel his body pressed into hers. It would be her cross, her death. Over his own head, he would feel the ghost of her hair; over his ribs, the swell of her breasts. His body would be her body. The wounds would be hers, the flesh and the blood.

He would take the nails into his hands. The spear would no longer pierce his side. He would feel its thrust into *her*. There would be a woman on the cross.

Sebastian raised his eyes to the place above the altar where the cross had left the pale glow of its mark on the adobe wall: "God of my fathers," he cried. "If she dies, let all the men of the Cristo-Rey die with her. If she lives, let her kingdom become my kingdom, her cross my cross."

 PART II

P R O L O G U E

T H E R E   W E R E   M A N Y versions sung by the troubadours who fled the valley of the Cristo-Rey, each in his own direction to a place where people would gather to hear the tale. All the songs agreed that the virgin Sidelle had been nailed in her bridal gown to the cross of the Cristo-Reys, and that Talifiero had been a witness to it.

According to one version, the harpist had been more than a witness; he had actually perpetrated the crime, not out of rage, but out of love, because she asked him to.

"Show me the courage of your love," she had said, "and nail me to this cross so that Sebastian Cristo-Rey and all his kin may know who it is that God the Father offers up as sacrifice."

This version was put out to explain why Talifiero had fled the country to a distant land. But more likely he had fled because his poetic sensibility could not bear the horror, or—others said—because he was ashamed to let anyone know that the romance of her beauty had been spoiled for him by the piercing of her hands.

More popular and credible was the version that said the father crucified his daughter. Certainly that is what the brothers believed when they rode out to avenge themselves for the desecration of their family cross. Up at the high end of the valley, they found Sidelle's father and his men, armed and ready for combat.

Every one of the brothers of the Cristo-Rey was slaughtered in the battle that ensued.

That is how the rebellion started. Once so many noblemen had been killed, the peasants thought there was no turning back. Though, if they had known how universally the brothers of the Cristo-Rey were despised among the landholders of that country, they would have thought otherwise.

Her father became their leader until he was captured and hung in the public plaza of the capital city. A great crowd gathered to witness the death of this man who had nailed his daughter to the cross. Afterward, the Emperor abolished the *droit du seieneur* throughout his empire. He granted amnesty to all combatants. The rebellion was effectively ended.

A version sung for commoners in the taverns celebrated the rape of the dissolute Sisters of the Cristo-Rey. It told of how Sidelle's father and his band of serfs rode to the hacienda, intending to complete their revenge by killing the last of the Christs, but Abraham and Sebastian had barred themselves inside the chapel with the girl. The serfs, whose rage was too impatient for the work of battering down such a thick door, contented themselves with pillaging the hacienda and raping the women of the Cristo-Rey.

According to a sweeter version, sung among monks and nuns and pious folk, no rape ever took place. These verses told of how the serfs tied the reins of their horses to the rail of the porch and stormed into the hacienda. In an upstairs room they were stopped by the sight of a bed with a circle of women kneeling in prayer around it.

On the bed lay Sidelle in her wedding dress, her hands open so that the bloody wounds could be seen. Her eyes were closed. But, in her delirium, she had raised up and reached out her arms. This action gave her such a resemblance to a certain bride of Christ lying in a glass case in the chapel of the Cristo-Rey, where these same men had sometimes gone to worship, that they were stunned into seeing her as a vision of the Blessed Virgin. They fell to their knees near the women to join them in a prayer for divine mercy.

Hearing this version sung years later by a guard outside the tomb (where the memoir from which our story is drawn)

Sebastian would wish that it had been so.

Whatever the truth, Sebastian Cristo-Rey would never know it. Except through hearsay, he would never know about the wildfire rebellion that nearly brought about the Emperor's overthrow. He would never know what caused the death of his brothers, and the return of his sisters to a life without men. All of this happened while he was in the chapel. For seven days after his brothers had pulled the nails from the hands of Sidelle and lifted her from the cross, he and his father nursed her there, keeping her out of sight from those who tried unsuccessfully to break in.

When Sebastian and his father ventured to open the door, when they walked the girl out into the sunlight, they would find that the world of the Cristo-Reys had changed entirely.

What was left of it.

O N E

THOUGH HE KEPT reminding himself that he had asked
God to destroy the Cristo-Reys only if Sidelle should die,
Sebastian could not forget that he had prayed for the death of
the men in his family. He was appalled at his strange power to
bring about catastrophe.

He wondered why he and his father had been spared. To
what purpose?

He tried to grieve the death of his brothers, but could not
summon any strong emotion.

Meanwhile, the most he could do was to try comforting his
father. But Abraham had gone to live in the ceremonial lodge
up in the woods on the hill, wishing to have no more converse
with anyone in the world, including his own last living son.
When Sebastian hiked up there and knocked, his father
shouted through the door that he did not want to see
Sebastian; this was his hermitage.

"Until you have brought me a grandson for the piercing of
his hands, I am no longer of this world. Leave me to my
prayers."

On his walk back to the hacienda, Sebastian found that he
was actually lighter of heart for not having to deal with his father. It seemed unlikely to Sebastian that he would ever have a
son, for he knew that he could never require the brides to line
up in front of the chapel again.

With me, he thought, the Cristo-Rey comes to an end. So be
it. Let history be rid of us.

There were no gay spirits in the house; the troubadours were
far gone.

The serfs—those who had survived the brushfire war—were back working their fields, but they were not friendly. Their rage at the crucifixion of Sidelle was still smoldering. Less to pacify them than to assuage his own guilt, Sebastian let it be known, before he learned that it was already law, that there would be no more bleeding of the virgins. To his surprise, this only made the men more bitter. Their one small chance to own land and to be free from serfdom had been taken away.

So he surrendered ownership of the land they farmed and promised to pay them fairly for their produce and labor. When he announced this news while standing on the porch with the men in a hostile pack on the lawn, glowering at him and expecting the worst for whatever reason he had summoned them, Sebastian could hardly believe how miraculously they changed. And when each one doffed his hat and took his turn coming to kneel at his feet and kiss his hand, Sebastian was not ashamed to let his serfs see him weep, then openly sob. Finally, he seized one of the old men who had just knelt, pulled him to his feet, and embraced him tightly.

He embraced all of his serfs at the moment of their freedom. The way their bodies, stinking so wonderfully of earth and sweat consoled him, he wondered if this intense gratitude they were feeling, this joy to be thus reconciled with him . . . whether his own gratitude for the forgiveness he now felt was not something very close to what was called love.

As the men walked away, he could see that they were still dazed by their good fortune, euphoric. It occurred to him that they belonged to him now as they had never belonged to him before.

His sisters and aunts, however, found the freeing of the serfs one more reason to act coldly toward him. That the men of the village should be rewarded when, as far as the women of the Cristo-Rey were concerned, they should all be flogged and castrated, was another affront. Another reason to go back into the dark.

The women of his house had taken to wearing long black dresses, like nuns, and to keeping their hair bound tightly in a knot behind their heads. Their behavior was even more austere than it had been during the period in their lives before they had discovered *amor*.

Whatever had happened during the week Sebastian and his father were hidden in the chapel with Sidelle, the women were filled with outrage against all men, dead or alive, stranger or kin. Nothing would induce them to tell him exactly why. Except for Maria Latona, who grudgingly attended to his needs and those of his father, they were not talking to men at all.

They would not let Sebastian near Sidelle. At night, they kept her locked away in the area at the back.

Maria Latona said that the girl was very sick; they were keeping vigil by her bed at night.

"Does she ask for me?"

"Ask for you?"

Maria Latona lifted her hands to heaven. She shook her head in disbelief.

During the day, Sidelle seemed their entire concern. The women were obsessed with healing her. Wherever she wandered in her daze, they surrounded her; they comforted and crooned over her; they called her their angel. They were like drones around a queen bee.

That she should recover from her fevers, regain her senses, and be entirely healed seemed a crucial and all-consuming concern.

They renamed their order *The Sisters of Sidelle*.

Sebastian spent much of his time in bed on his back, reading and memorizing the poems of St. John of the Cross. He would lay his book aside sometimes and go into a kind of trance, imagining that he was John come into the cell of Saint Teresa in the middle of the night to pray with her. He relived over and over again a moment when they were no longer able to struggle against desire, and fell into each others' arms.

One morning, Maria Latona shook him from one of these very intense erotic trances. She pointed to his clothes on the floor, signaling him to get dressed and go downstairs immediately. When he did so, he found soldiers at the door ready to take him away.

The women were not there to plead his cause. They had hidden themselves in the back of the house. Maria Latona was the only member of the household to witness how the hands of the Christ were tied behind his back and he was marched to a waiting carriage. Looking over his shoulder, Sebastian kept hoping that Sidelle would somehow appear on the porch to see that it was his turn to suffer.

In front of the emperor's tribunal, he was found guilty of taking a girl's virginity without the consent of her father. This offense was not usually considered serious if the girl was a commoner, but in the law books it was, after all, listed as a cardinal offense, and it had caused a peasant uprising, suppressed only after the sacrifice of a divine right that the noblemen of this small country had been the last in the Christian world to enjoy. The Cristo-Rey must surely understand that he was no longer very much loved among the landed gentry.

"To be frank, Sebastian Cristo-Rey," spoke the judge at the tribunal, nodding toward the Commander of the Imperial Army who was twisting his mustache and glowering as he watched the proceedings, "there are those even so vehement as to want to see you executed in the public plaza here in our capital city where all who revile you may enjoy the sight of your death as they did the death of the man whose daughter you stole from his keeping. Do you have anything to say?"

"I will acknowledge that through my vanity and pride," Sebastian said with a serenity that surprised him, "I have brought about a great calamity." And then, relieved that his moment had come, he felt a sudden rush of ardor, and heard himself cry out, "I ask only that I be allowed to die on the cross."

The emperor's judge laughed loudly while the papal nuncio looked toward the ceiling as if pleading with God to ignore such an affront.

"But, my poor Cristo-Rey, surely you see that your vanity and pride are greater than ever. They have reached monstrous proportions. Better we should have you buried alive than allow you to die like the Son of God Himself. Where did a player like you ever muster such spiritual presumption?"

The secular judge lay a hand on the nuncio's arm and looked down from the high bench with a contemptuous smile.

"My dear Cristo-Rey, even if we took seriously this impulse of yours for a dramatic repentance, do you really think that we could afford to perform a true crucifixion on the one who plays our Christ? This is an age of enlightenment. Our laws are themselves governed by very practical concerns. You happen to be a great attraction to visitors from abroad. Your crucifixions bring wealth to our country as long as they do not cause a scandal. Already, through an unseemly show, you have come too close to dying on the cross. There will be no more playing to our women's unfortunate attachment to the tragic sense of life. Easter is just as much your business as is the crucifixion. Indeed more so, considering the general disinterest among the natives of this land in our Lord's resurrection.

"The court has agreed that you require a humbling, lest the entire race of the Cristo-Reys become extinct.

"As for your having tupped a girl against her father's will, why should we punish ourselves for that small crime of yours, our Emperor asks? The archbishop has suggested a much more suitable punishment in keeping with the new laws which your actions have forced us to institute, voiding the divine right of the bleeder.

"The Emperor asks that, for the sake of peace in this land, and so that the people will be satisfied that justice has been done . . ."

The judge hesitated. It was such a scandal to require this of a Cristo-Rey, even one who had so entirely disgraced himself.

The nuncio spoke up: "The Emperor desires that henceforth the Cristo-Reys submit themselves to the laws of the church and that, as your punishment and penance, you marry this girl who carries the venerable marks of the stigmata in her hands. He urges you to get to work having children by her so that the lineage of the Cristo-Reys be hastily replenished."

Sebastian felt a rising of hope when he heard this wonderful sentence. He smiled ruefully, however, and told the judge he was quite sure the girl would never marry the likes of him.

"It is not the prerogative of such a child to choose," the judge said indignantly.

"Indeed not," pronounced the nuncio. "I myself, at tomorrow's sunrise, will be ready to accompany you home to perform that sacrament."

Thus it was that Sebastian was condemned by religious and secular law to do what he had always dreamed of doing, but never imagined that he really could.

T W O

THE NEXT MORNING, he found himself riding home
with the nuncio. They were escorted by soldiers and followed
by a contingent of servants. Despite the screaming of his sisters
and aunts, Sebastian's bride was dressed once more in her
wedding gown, and taken to the chapel of the Cristo-Reys
where, under the cross on which she had hung, the vows were
pronounced while the sisters, dressed as bridesmaids, stood behind Sidelle, waiting to catch her if she should fall into a
swoon.

Before the nuncio spoke the words of the ceremony, Sebastian turned to look at Sidelle. He could not see her face under
the veil, even though she turned it towards him. Was she
scowling? Weeping?

"Forgive me," he whispered.

To his utter surprise, she slipped her wounded hand under
his arm.

When answers were required, she replied quite sanely that
she would take him as her lawfully wedded husband, and be
obedient to him until they were parted by death.

He was astonished by her compliance.

Astonished later when, as the custom required, they lay side
by side in what had been his father's bedroom, under a quilt,
she and he in their nightgowns, on their backs, arm against
arm, staring at the ceiling.

"I will never violate you," he said. "You need not be afraid of
me at all."

Her hand, icy cold, found his and held onto it. Her finger nails cut deep into his skin. He endured it. A sickness, like a flow of hot poison, surged down through his loins into his legs and feet. He felt a fluttering in his chest. His throat gagged, as if he were being strangled. His scalp tingled, his arms burned.

His hand grew so hot that it melted the coldness of the hand he held. Her finger nails dug right down into the bones on the back of his hand. One finger pushed hard through the hole of his stigma. She made a strange sound. He shuddered.

After some time, during which he felt his body undergoing other sickly changes, she pulled her finger out of his wound. She took hold of his hand again, this time more gently.

For a long time, he lay there wide awake, alert with all his senses to this illness whose exact source he could not locate inside his body. He searched for it in his arms, his legs, his loins, listening to the flow of his veins, attending with something like alarm to the quieting of his breath, until it seemed he was hardly breathing at all.

He could no longer hear the beat of his heart. But he could feel it pulsing in his finger tips.

What was so terribly wrong?

Sebastian underwent something like panic. He wondered if perhaps he was dying. Yet his body was neither too warm nor too cold. In some way, this was a pleasant disease, like the euphoria he sometimes felt after a fever had subsided.

Then his mind blossomed. He understood.

He was not sick at all.

He had simply not recognized this feeling for what it was, not having known it for so many years. With a pure and peaceful clarity, he smiled, and felt his body sink calmly, deeply into the mattress.

Her ankle, leg, hip, shoulder were warm against his own. He turned his face to inhale the fragrance of her hair. She was still

holding his hand, her wound pressed into his.
 Happiness, he thought.
 It was very dark now.
 He felt her hand relax and fall asleep.
 Happiness. This was happiness.

 THREE

DURING THE DAYS, the sisters kept her to themselves.
But nights, Sidelle obediently came to his bed, lay close by his
side, and even conversed with him in a friendly, detached way,
no doubt grateful (he thought) that he did not force her, or
even expect her to allow him a husband's usual rights.

He asked her one night why she had not simply kept silent
during the wedding ceremony, since she had been stood up at
the altar against her will. Why had she spoken the wedding
vows as if so sincerely?

Because she meant them, she said. She wished to be a wife
to the Cristo-Rey.

"But why?"

"That is the only way to defeat you," she said.

That silenced him for a time.

But then she reached over and patted his hand. She said that
marrying him and sharing his bed was also a penance for all
the horror she had caused: the slaughter of his brothers, the
war, the death of her father and other men she loved, the dis-
appearance of the 'boy' she had been enamored of, the misery
of the women: she had caused it all, and caused him undue
suffering too, because she had known that he, as much as she,
was the victim of a custom neither of them had wanted to
obey.

"But it was I who was the cause of it all," he protested.

"You were quite noble at a certain time," she said

"What of Talifiero?"

"He was enamored of my purity. He could not have loved a
girl who bore such wounds, seeing that his love had put them

there. As for wanting to marry me. That was a ruse. He wanted to romance me forever, which pleased my father, since I needed to be kept at home where my mother could come to train me in her art."

"Her art? What art was that?"

Sighing, she squeezed his hand in such a way that he wondered whether, if he rose up on one elbow and touched her shoulder she might not reach her arms up and pull him to her breast.

But he could not.

Having learned that Talifiero had never taken her maidenhead, that she was still a virgin, he had vowed to himself that he would let her remain so as long as she only meant to yield to him out of mere sense of duty. She must truly love him, truly desire him. He would wait for an unmistakable signal of her passion, even if he had to wait for a very long time, even if it meant he was never to enjoy her sexually at all.

She let go of his hand, turned on her side. The touch of her buttocks aroused him.

He remembered what his father had told him long ago about the goddess Sidelle. He wished he had listened more carefully.

He knew that before the advent of the conquistadors the country had been a gigantic forest from one ocean to the other. Except for the few villages of fishermen who lived along the rugged coast, the people received their sustenance from the fruits, nuts and bark of the trees, and from the animals and birds who live in their branches. They worshipped the goddess of the forest, whose name the conquerors pronounced as Sidelle, and whom all female children were named after, just as Christian girls were named after Maria.

There were certain old and very powerful trees around which the forest villages were built, and these were the trees in which Sidelle's winged spirit was known to alight when it was time to be worshipped.

When the conquerors landed, their commander, later the first of those who called himself 'emperor,' sought to claim the power of the tree spirit as his own by forcefully taking the daughter of the chief priestess as his wife.

The sacred trees were all cut down. Churches were built on the same ground under which their roots had fed. For a woman to officiate at any religious function was forbidden. It was declared by the priests of the newly installed religion that the pagan goddess had been destroyed. Trees would be worshipped no longer. A god whose dwelling was high in the heavens would henceforth rule the land with love and mercy.

The churches thrived, but not because the natives worshipped Christ at all. Christ was for those whose religion had been imported from abroad. The natives adapted their religion to the churches by secretly worshipping the cross itself, which they came to revere as the dead tree in whose body the spirits of their martyred tree goddess, and the martyred sky god of their conquerors slept to await rebirth at a time when the strife was ended and the goddess and god were wed in the branches of The Tree of Life.

Those who continued openly to practice the religion of the trees were burned at the stake; but for more than a century Sidelle was still worshipped in secret, not only through veneration of the cross there in the places where the roots of the sacred trees still clung to the earth beneath the Christian altars, but in a secret grove as yet undiscovered by the Inquisition: a grove where a certain rugged mountain oak still stood, one that Sidelle's spirit had visited many times, and to which a few remaining priestesses, whose identities had been kept hidden, guided pilgrims of the old faith, that they might pray for release of Sidelle from the cross, pray for her spirit's escape to this sacred tree whose branches were waiting to embrace her.

Meanwhile, the conquerors—a mixture of Spaniards, Frenchmen, Englishmen, took possession of the women of that land, just as they had the land itself, through their 'divine right.' The women and the land were regarded as offerings of God from His Divine Creation to redeem men from their ensnarement within the treacherous realm of nature, and to raise them above nature to positions of power and well-being.

A vast lumbering industry became their 'empire.' Their bastard children, in the spirit of Christian enterprise, joined the work of raping the forests. For great distances all around, trees were felled to clear land for the villages and sawmills where millions of logs were floated down the rivers, sawed into beams and boards, and loaded on barges for shipment abroad.

The country prospered. Many *seiñeurs* set up their haciendas on the lands they were ravaging.

The empire literally went to ruin.

There was a rebellion accompanied by a resurgence of the old religion.

A group of rebels gathered in the sacred grove to declare war against the regime. They vowed their allegiance to the holy tree that stood on the top of the mountain, rising from the central plateau on one of the last tracts of virgin forest that had not yet been attacked by the lumbering industry.

On this mountain, the rebels decided to make their stand. Armies were raised against them, but soldiers moving in ranks and dragging cannons were no match for the rebels, who fought a guerilla war using the trees for protection. For several decades, they held off the imperial troops until the emperor finally grew so exasperated that he destroyed the pagan force by setting fire to the forest during the driest season of the year.

The fire raged to the very top of the mountain. The sacred tree died with its people.

Soon afterward, the lumbering industry came to an end.

From cutting down the trees, the haciendas had become fabulously rich. Indeed, all the people had prospered. But now the forests, except around the valley of the Cristo-Reys, had been decimated. The country was poor and dusty. Its only remaining resource of any value lay underground in the black bones of the ancient trees; and the coal industry had added a darker dust, tearing up the land, spreading a black cloud over it so that the once-beautiful colonial cities were covered with soot.

With the opening of the mines and the stripping of the land, the grave of the ancient goddess had been torn open, the rebel legend said. Her sacred bones were being stolen from the ground to fuel the engines of further destruction.

While nailed to his cross, Sebastian had often looked out over the putrid landscapes of this or that mining town (the mining towns were the ones that could afford his crucifixion) and he had wondered whether humankind deserved to be saved; whether a more truly heroic act might not be to refuse the crucifixion, to announce that the Christ no longer considered mankind worth redeeming, since the redemption of men meant the death of the earth.

What a pleasure it would be to delay until the city of his crucifixion was packed with visitors, and then . . . perhaps before Pontius Pilate at the trial . . . still better, on the way to Calvary . . . to drop his cross and look around him at the industrial desolation, and to say, "No, no, I will not die for the sake of this."

He had taken a perverse delight sometimes, while hanging on the cross, to think this way, with contempt for the men who were bleeding the world below. But then they would crucify him against his will, perhaps even leave him on the cross to die, as a warning to other Cristo-Reys. For refusing to act out God's death for mankind, he would have to endure a real death. He knew he was not that courageous.

These were notions he had played with in his head before Sidelle was nailed to his cross. They seemed fatuous, grandiose, now that the contempt he felt was for himself. He was the one who was not worth redeeming.

Yet he prayed that somehow, before he gave up the cross, he

would be blessed, through God's grace, with the joy of having Sidelle yearn for him as he yearned for her; that she would open herself to him ardently, receiving his seed into her womb.

His sisters had been trying to impress on him lately that his only hope for awakening Sidelle's passion was in somehow helping to give back what had been plundered, not just from the bodies of the women, but from the body of the goddess they worshipped: from the forests, the earth.

But they spoke in riddles he could not decipher. They were hinting at events he must be ready for, as if they wanted him to know a secret for winning Sidelle's heart which they did not dare divulge.

FOUR

ONE OF SEBASTIAN'S UNCLES had told him about a girl who had been raped and then repeatedly stabbed when she cried out for help. After recovering from her wounds, the girl went about as if nothing had happened. For more than a year, she was as cheerful as ever. She even allowed a wedding to be arranged, and behaved quite normally on her wedding night. Then, one morning, as she lay beside her husband, she began to scream, and had been screaming ever since, totally insane.

The uncle had told this story when Sebastian was still a boy awaiting the ritual of his stigmatization. "It is best not to swallow the pain," the uncle had said. "When they cut your hands open, go ahead and scream."

Even though the story of the girl who was stabbed made a powerful impression on Sebastian, he could not remember having screamed, could not remember that there was even any pain. But sometimes, having heard horror stories from his brothers about their own excruciating agony at the hands of their father and grandfather, Sebastian wondered whether he had not simply forgotten the pain because it was so great.

Would Sidelle wake up one morning screaming, or had the women guided her safely through the period of her mild insanity. Should he not encourage her to talk about her crucifixion, before the poison of its memory sank too deep?

Late one night, he decided to risk the question:

"I have been trying to understand. Could it really have been your father who nailed you to the cross?"

"My father adored me."

"So it was not him? Was it the harpist, then?"

She thought about this for a long time.

"My Talifiero could not have been that cruel even if he had wanted to be. Whoever it was, I never saw his face."

"But the candles were still burning, were they not?"

"He seized me from behind. I was so terrified that I closed my eyes. When I opened them, he was already driving a spike into my hand. I was blinded by the pain."

"It was not your father, and not your lover. Who, then? You don't think it was I!"

"All I can be sure of is that whoever nailed me to the cross did so because of you. Because of all the Cristo-Reys."

She rolled over with her back to him, and would not answer any more questions.

On another night, he confessed that he found her more intelligent than he was.

"I can feel you here beside me always thinking about something, turning something over in your head. What is it?"

She gave no answer.

He said that he had always found the peasants and common people brighter than the nobility; they knew how to cope with so much more. They cleared their own land, built their own houses, birthed their own children, witched their own water, could repair whatever was broken, understood everything about animal husbandry; they could plant, prune, harvest, hunt, trap, create systems of irrigation; they knew how to heal with herbs and incantations; they created their own music, their own dances, their own feasts and ceremonies, their own sports. The more he thought about it, the more bewildering it was that they were the subjects of people who knew how to do relatively nothing.

She laughed bitterly.

"Our independence terrifies you, doesn't it? You need to enslave all that peasant know-how of ours, or you'd be helpless.

Left to your own devices, you of the *seigñeurs* would die of disease and starvation within a few years. There must be something too passive about us, too acquiescent. Perhaps we feel
even more pity than fear for you. I don't know. Perhaps you've
put too much of our blood in your veins, or ours in yours;
you've turned too many of us into bastards who don't know
who to be loyal to any more. Perhaps we needed the god you
brought us just as badly as you need the goddess, the empress
who ruled before you came. This I can assure you, husband,
we can endure your crucifixion and the strange story that goes
with it, but there can only be a resurrection when we regain
our own story. When the land belongs to us to care for in a
proper way again."

"But nothing is stopping you. I have returned the land of this
valley to your people."

"That was a kind but sentimental act. I'm talking about
when the entire country *truly* belongs to us."

"I hear your father speaking."

She turned her face to him, and scowled: "Listen more
closely. You are hearing *me!*"

He considered what she had said about a resurrection of her
people, her land. What the judge at his trial had said was true:
among the common people — those who were not visitors from
abroad, or nobility, but grounded still in the old pre-Christian
ways — little heed had been paid to Easter morning. On Good
Friday, the people all turned out to grieve the death of God.
Men, women, children, from the richest to the poorest, natives, mixed bloods, those from the most distant lands, they all
shed tears along his path. But on the day of his resurrection,
the natives had already gone back to their daily chores.
Clearly, none of them believed that Christ ever rose. If Christ
was to become their god, then Christ would remain on the
cross until they were free.

The churches, though full of flowers at Easter, were empty of
the people who knew how to garden this land, who knew how

to cultivate beautiful flowers: the people whose bodies and whose lands were being bled.

Sebastian had always played out his exit from the tomb to the much smaller gathering of those who claimed the bloodlines and the overseas heritage of the conquerors.

"And since I've given your people back their land," he said, "why could there not be a resurrection, at least here in this valley?"

She raised up on one elbow. "Do you mean what you say, Sebastian?"

He did not exactly understand the conversations they had been having lately, but it thrilled him so to have heard her for the first time call him simply 'Sebastian' that he answered without hesitation, "I do." Then he added, more out of gallantry than conviction, "My wish is to obey my wife's every command."

"Would you worship her then?"

She looked down at him quite sweetly, her high cheeked face, with those exotic eyes so radiantly hopeful that he had to laugh at the way he could please her sometimes without really knowing why.

"I have worshipped you, Sidelle, since first I saw the mystery of your face."

"I don't mean *me*," she scolded. "I mean *her*."

He threw back the covers, got onto his knees there on the bed, and pressed his forehead to her stomach, grateful that she not only kept him there, but was pushing her fingers through his hair.

"I worship Sidelle. The girl, the woman, my wife." He reached down tentatively to lay a hand on her thigh. "The virgin, alas."

She tugged at his hair with playful reproach. "I do not wish you to blaspheme by saying you worship me. Acknowledge that you worship the one who *lives* in me."

She let go of his hair, took firm hold of his head, turned it sideways so that his ear was pressed to her stomach.

He looked up at her with a wondering eye. Did she mean that he should worship the goddess in her as she imagined he worshipped the image of God in man?

He remembered when out there in front of the chapel the brides were lined up, and it had first dawned on him that he might marry her, how the thought had passed through his mind: despite all their sins, it was right that a Cristo-Rey be married to the name Sidelle. From the time his ancestors had begun to purchase vast tracts of forest around the valley to save the trees from being cut down, they had shown a certain reverence for the name Sidelle.

Whatever hostilities their serfs might have felt, due to the injustices perpetrated by the Cristo-Reys, he knew that the people of the valley had always appreciated their lords for resisting the pressures of the lumber *seigñeurs*.

"Are you listening?" she scolded. "Even in jest, to say you worship me is a sin."

"The one who lives in you," he conceded, and opened one eye to scrutinize her. She was of pure native blood, he was certain of that, or she would not have been named Sidelle.

He closed his eyes and let his head sink into the softness of her stomach while he pondered the meaning of her name.

She grabbed him by the shoulders. She shook him playfully.

"Lives in *all* women," she smiled, then slapped him on the cheek. "Sebastian Cristo-Rey, when thoughts start rolling around in that innocent mind of yours . . . what are you thinking?"

"It occurred to me how your mother is a priestess, and that already when I took you, you too—"

She reached down, snatched his wrist, and threw his hand away from where it had been pressing on her hip.

"You did not take me. I was forced on you, just as you were forced on me. We are both unfortunates."

"I count myself blessed."

"Do you now? We'll see how blessed you turn out to be. Finish what you were saying. It occurred to you . . . what?"

"It occurred to me that I had been forced, against my will, of course, to receive a holy woman as my bride."

She looked at him with astonishment. "Which of your sisters told you this?"

He put a finger over his lips, shook his head.

Her mouth trembled.

"They were sworn to secrecy," she pouted. "And I am not a holy woman. I am a priestess merely. Like you, a means of worship, nothing more. Like my mother, I am an actress. But, thanks to you, of such short term that I have never even had the opportunity to try my craft."

She sat up and laughed ruefully.

"Try your craft on me," he said. "Teach me your religion."

She said that she could not go back to being what her mother was: a woman who guided pilgrims up to the sacred tree and chanted prayers. If that was all that she knew how to do, she could have taken him to a place not far from his own ceremonial lodge where God bore no wounds other than the wounds in which the birds and squirrels made their nests. She could have taken him up into his own hills and shown him where the goddess still lived in a beautiful tree with roots that were drinking from the earth before the conquerors had ever come.

"No," she said, "I feel now that our religious destinies are entwined, and that I must be your wife in every way so that I can entwine my life entirely with yours. That is my instinct."

"Entwine in *every* way?"

He made a feeble effort to reach for her. She brushed his hand away.

"Soon," she murmured. "I promise you."

F I V E

SHE WAS STILL ASLEEP when Sebastian awoke, donned his purple robe, and went out onto the balcony to listen to the birds. Not the birds in cages, for they had all been released on the day he was inspired to free the serfs.

No, the birds he heard were singing in the orchard, as cheerful in their freedom as the workers whose own whistling could be heard in the vineyards. The sun was shining brightly. A pale violet mist still billowed off the ground.

He looked over his shoulder at Sidelle, pleased to see how peacefully she was sleeping, her mouth relaxed, almost smiling.

Her hand, lying open on the sheet, showed its wound most beautifully in a shaft of sunlight.

Her stigmata had been impressively healed by his father's ministrations. She also had worn plugs for a time inside the holes so that they would not seal. Abraham Cristo-Rey had treated her as he might have his own son. But none of the men had ever borne such a beauteous stigma as this that pulsed on the pillow in the palm of her hand, pink like the petal of a rose.

He looked up to the hills from whence the scent of pine needles was swept toward him on the breeze.

On the carriage road that wound down into the valley from the highway, he saw three men round a bend. More men followed.

Who were they?

They were not dressed as peasants, nor as noblemen. From this far distance, they appeared to be wearing the bloused trousers and shirts of working men from one of the towns. He counted eleven of them. They carried no banner. Some kind of pilgrimage, though.

Why were they coming here?

The only time that pilgrims ever visited the hacienda was later in the year, in early November, when the Cristo-Rey traditionally received emissaries come to petition, and to offer inducements for the honor of having him choose their town or city as the site of his crucifixion. But such pilgrims arrived by carriage, richly and colorfully dressed. These clearly had some other purpose.

They disappeared around another bend. He watched for a long time, waiting for them to appear on the bottom of the road that passed through the orchard. The peach trees had lost enough of their leaves so that the men could vaguely be seen through the branches when they finally did appear. They were hardly moving at all now, and they were . . . what?

Were they crawling?

Yes, in a single file–he could see them vaguely–they were on their knees one in front of the other. They had removed their shirts, rolled them up, and tied them around their waists.

"Sidelle. Come look."

SIX

THE MEN WERE JUST crawling out from behind the trees into the clear when she arrived in her robe to stand behind him.

"Are they your people?" he asked

"No," she cried. "Oh, please, no."

They were crawling slowly across the gravel of the road toward the hacienda.

"Whips?" she asked. "Are those whips?"

She turned away. She ran off.

Yes, as they came closer he could see how they did carry little whips, just like the ones he had seen among the penitents at his own crucifixions: the whips that were sold on the path to Calvary. And the men down there wore the same crowns of thorns sold to pilgrims during Holy Week.

They were powerfully built, huge of shoulder, real brutes.

He knew what they had come for.

They had come to nail him to his cross.

He had been expecting them. He had fantasized their coming. Desired it sometimes.

Now that they were here, he found that he was only a little afraid, less than when he played his usual role, though he knew that he would not be taken down this time: He would be left up there above the altar of his chapel to die.

He even felt a slight rise of anticipation.

But quickly he fell into a wistful regret for having come so close to knowing the love and sexual passion of Sidelle, even though she was the very woman for whose crucifixion they had come to avenge themselves.

He became aware that his knees began to shake. But his mind felt at peace.

There was plenty of time to prepare; they were moving so slowly out there. He wished she had stayed beside him. He wanted to thank Sidelle for having given him, if only briefly and tentatively, intimations of what a wife might be.

She had given him sufficient happiness so that he knew he would die with love in his heart. He wanted to tell her that. But she had fled.

She was already down in the cloister, hiding among the sisters, and there seemed to be a stone lodged hard in his throat. It stayed stuck there even as he stood watching the pilgrims inch their way toward the house.

They were led by a bull of a man. He looked oddly familiar. Down from the crown of thorns, blood streamed over the man's nose and cheeks, into his beard. His trousers had been ripped to shreds, the knees raw and bloody.

Despite this awful appearance, the man's expression was one of rapture, brought to grimaces of ecstasy each time the man behind him flailed at his back.

All but the last in line was bloodying the back of the one in front of him.

When the procession had stopped at the foot of the porch stairs, the one at their head raised his perspiring face to look up at Sebastian.

"Cristo-Rey?" he called, almost laughing. He nodded over his shoulder at the fellow behind him.

That second man in line leaned out, grinning in some kind of delirious ecstasy, his face also streaming with blood. Sebastian was horrified to see his brother Roman; not Roman himself, but his brother looking out through the face of the other man.

Sebastian understood.

These were the ghosts of his brothers.

His eyes filled with tears, he was so suddenly mortified for having loved them so little. Had they come to haunt him?

He wiped his tears on his sleeve. He could not recognize the others. Squinting into the sunlight, he could only see that they were leering up at him almost obscenely. He saw the leers of certain saints. The paintings on tin brought over by the conquistadors from the tragic chapels of Spain depicted saints with faces like these.

"I am he," said Sebastian, though no sound came out.

He turned his face away, and looked toward the chapel. He could not face these masks of his own murdered brothers, so huge was the remorse that ached in his chest. He felt as if his heart was spilling out blood. Sebastian looked inward. He saw himself already on the cross in the candlelit chapel of the Cristo-Rey. He saw his brothers down there in their usual pews, and was grateful to feel a fierce surge of affection for the mischief in their faces. He recognized their loyalty, their brotherly strength. He looked out at the men who knelt there, but saw them inside his own mind as his brothers loving him and forgiving him, accepting the love of the one they had nailed to the cross.

"Cristo-Rey, don't you recognize us?"

"My . . . brothers?" Sebastian asked so softly he knew he could no be heard.

"The butchers of La Paz!" the man shouted now gleefully. "Don't you remember? You lifted me right over your head and threw me out of the ring."

The man clasped his hands fervently to his heart. "We thought, since we were your friends, we might be the first—"

Sebastian blinked. He looked at the men again.

"The Azteca? Is it you?"

"All of us," cried a man farther up the line.

And another, beaming: "We have come to ask if we might be the first to see her, and to worship her, Sebastian Cristo-Rey."

"Worship her?"

The Azteca's eyes were closed, as if he had already begun

this worship, as if he were thanking God for having brought him safely to a shrine. A trickle of blood flowed out from under his knee across the flagstone on which he knelt.

Seeing Sebastian's consternation, the man last in line dropped his whip and, grinning, shouted out gleefully, "He means the girl who hung upon the cross, señor!"

 SEVEN

WHEN SEBASTIAN ESCORTED THEM to the garden of the cloister where Sidelle and the sisters had prepared themselves, the butchers found Sidelle seated in a chair of stretched cowhide, in front of the fountain in her wedding dress. On her long raven-black hair, glinting with blue against the water that gushed behind and above it from the mouth of a stone fish, she wore a crown of thorns lightly placed so as not to cut into her brow. Strands of heavenly blue morning glories had been entwined over and under the thorns. Her bare feet rested on the grass that encircled the fountain. Her forearms lay on the arms of the chair, with hands draped down over the front so that her stigmata seemed to radiate sunlight.

Sebastian had never seen her looking so regally happy, or so much in command. Her beaming face contrasted with the stark, tight-mouthed expressions of the Sisters.

Hands in their laps, fingers entwined with orange-beaded rosaries, The Sisters of Sidelle sat in their black habits and winged hats, stiff and straight and somewhat self-satisfied, on high-backed wooden chairs in a semicircle around the back of the fountain.

The butchers had fallen to their knees, one behind the other, between the hedges along the flagstone path that led to the throne of the one whose blessing they sought.

Sebastian, watching from under the arcade, was intrigued to see with what imaginative grace Sidelle improvised the kind of religious ceremony he had thought only a Cristo-Rey would have the style and finesse to carry off when he was playing the Christ.

It was obvious to him now that she had indeed been bred to the role of priestess. Sebastian, remembering his Magdalenes with a sigh of nostalgia, felt even a little envious to see the butchers so deliriously awed in Sidelle's presence.

As each one bloodied the stones with his crawling, and finally reached the grass, where the two parallel streaks of blood now glinted against the green, he would stop close enough so that he could almost touch his forehead to the hands that were resting on her knees. She would lift her hand to his mouth, let him take hold of it, and kiss the scar.

Then she would unstick the crown of thorns from the penitent's head, place it on the rim of the fountain and, reaching back to dip her hand in the water, wash the blood and sweat from his brow. She would dip her hand again, waft it in the water, bring it out palm up and, having let the water trickle through her wound upon the man's head, turn her hand over and perform a kind of baptism; after which she would bid him rise and go in peace.

When all the pilgrims, having received their blessing, were standing to either side of Sebastian under the arcades, their leader spoke for all of them.

He thanked Sidelle. He said that everyone throughout the land, having heard how the signs of her Second Coming could be seen in her palms, knew now that it was true. She was with them again. He said that he and the men of his gild were grateful that they had been asked to go seek her out first, thanks to their friendship with the Christ; and that, when they had testified that all the signs were true, they knew that others would also come, and they devoutly hoped she would receive them.

She said that she would be expecting these other pilgrims. She would indeed receive them. Next time with proper ceremony, in the chapel where her cross now hung.

That evening, after the men were gone, she invited Sebastian at last to come make love with her.

But he could not.

How could he explain this fear he felt? She had truly become like a kind of goddess, too intimidating, too awesome to approach so intimately.

How could a sinner such as he be the lover of someone he so revered?

EIGHT

MANY GROUPS OF PILGRIMS visited the chapel of the Cristo-Reys. Sometimes they came in families, men, women and children together; sometimes they were only men; most often they were all women.

She received them seated in the chancel in the bishop's chair. It pleased her, as a sign of her martyrdom, that fresh straw should be scattered on the tiles.

In a semi-circle of high-backed chairs, carved with images of the Marys crying out in grief, sat the Sisters of Sidelle, but no longer dressed in black. They too wore bridal gowns, their hair adorned with wildflowers and combed down loosely over their shoulders. They were beautiful to gaze upon by the light of the many candelabra, but not nearly as beautiful as Sidelle, who now wore a much more elaborate white silk gown sparkling with jewels and spread out in a great circular swirl at her feet.

But at first the penitents looked neither to the Sisters nor to Sidelle as they dropped to their knees. They looked up to the bride of Christ, nailed to the cross above the altar. She was very small to be hung on such a large cross. It seemed to Sebastian that the virgin (the doll he had removed from the glass case and nailed up there) kept receding farther and farther into the wood.

They gazed at the virgin on the cross, crossing themselves repeatedly. They wept and wailed. Sometimes they implored the image for mercy, or for special favors. Sometimes to Sebastian, looking over his left shoulder from where he sat in the choir loft at the organ, it sounded as if the men and women down there were howling like a pack of wolves.

Only when he began to play the organ or the harp—sacred tunes Talifiero had taught him—did the penitents quiet down and look to Sidelle, who opened her arms to welcome them.

They left their pews to approach timidly, one at a time, receiving her blessing with star-struck eyes.

When all had kissed her wounds, the group would leave the chapel to walk through the orchard for a time, ritually touching the trunks of the trees.

These ceremonies took place almost every day. Sometimes just a few pilgrims arrived. Sometimes, when Sidelle and Sebastian donned their robes and walked out to their balcony before breakfast, they saw that a great many people had already arrived, and were asleep all over the lawn.

The Sisters could not have been happier now, busy as they were providing for the needs of everyone. Maria Latona was in charge, though she moved more slowly as the months passed. She had ceased to wear white like the other women of the Cristo-Rey, for she was growing large with child.

She brought much joy to the household by giving birth to a boy in mid-winter.

Sidelle, who had learned midwifery from her mother, delivered the infant. Somehow, she was so aroused by holding the infant that she no longer held back in showing her desire for her husband.

It seemed to him that she must love him dearly now for having risked the wrath of all his ancestors, turning the family chapel over to her, as he had, supporting her, helping her, guiding her sometimes as he did in responding to so many, staving off the outrage of his father, who stormed down hoping to put a stop to it all, and was sent back sulking to his hermitage.

Sebastian knew that she was pleased with him, and wanted to reward him as a woman can. Yet, when he lay by her side, he found himself ignoring her hints. He pretended to be unaware that she would have him now, even though he yearned for her constantly.

He was dismayed, yet could not make his lips approach hers. He could not lift a hand to touch her breasts.

So they lay side by side, night after night, and talked, and slept.

He looked forward to the time when he would remove the doll bride from the cross, let the Sisters lay the doll back in her glass case. He would take the cross down, remove the golden spikes, carry the cross out of the chapel, feeling its serous weight again, lift it up, tie it to the top of the carriage, and travel with it far away to the city where he was to be crucified.

Once he was gone to his crucifixion, he knew he would have time to think, as one can only think when left alone. Perhaps he would understand why it was that he had lost his male power with this woman so admired, perhaps too much revered.

He told her how much he would miss her while he was gone.

Her face lit up. "Take me with you, Sebastian. Let the people see that we're together, and that all is well."

"You'll stay here and you'll rest. If any pilgrims come, I'll have the sisters send them away." He smiled mischievously. "You cannot hold court until I bring you back your cross."

"Please, Sebastian. I want to go with you. Didn't you say you need someone to play the angel? Am I not your angel?"

"Yes. Yes, you are."

"Then let me be the angel at your tomb."

Such a magical scene to imagine! Sidelle stepping forth from the tomb. His own radiant lady. His holy lady announcing his resurrection.

"O, how I wish you could," he said. "But it is simply out of the question."

"Why?"

"Too dangerous this year. There are men who truly revile me now. Women too. Who knows what they might do."

"Then you *must* take me."

"I will not."

"When they see me at your side, they won't be angry any more."

"They will be angrier than ever."

"Because they love me, they will let me teach them how to love you again. Let me show the world what a good man you have become. Let me be your angel."

"Impossible."

NINE

NOT LONG AFTERWARD, Sebastian was seated at the dining table, still conversing with the women after Sidelle had excused herself. They were telling him of a lovely dress they had fashioned for her. "Hurry to your room," one of them said, "she wants to show it to you."

When he opened the bedroom door, the room was pitch dark. She had blown out the candles. Was she already in bed so early? No.

The dressing room door opened on a circle of golden light.

Blinded, he shut his eyes, opened them again, and saw the glow move toward him, stop.

He held his breath.

An angel was standing there, holding a lamp in front of her. An angel complete with open wings, along which waves of shadow moved up and down, making them seem to waft backward and forward high against the wall, and over the ceiling.

An aura of copper light, radiating shafts of gold and black, surrounded her. Blue-green waves streaked across the hair she had brushed down over her breasts. She was wearing some kind of bare-shouldered gown of . . . what? Of a shimmering yellow silk, it must have been. She was standing on her toes, turning this way and that.

"I hope you like it, my dear husband. The Sisters made it for me." She cleared her throat, and spoke in a loud, ringing voice: *"You mustn't be afraid. I know you are looking for Jesus, who was nailed to the cross. He is not here."*

She chuckled in a particularly soft way of hers, like a dove cooing, and set the lantern on the bedside table.

"First, take off my wings," she whispered, "before they catch fire."

He unfastened her wings. He lay them on the carpet.

"Take me," she pleaded.

He swallowed hard. Proud to be so suddenly aroused, he approached her boldly.

She pushed her hands out, palms up.

She said tenderly, "I meant . . . I meant, take me with you."

He stepped back, forlorn.

Her expression softened almost to pity.

"You may take me that way too, Sebastian. But promise first that you'll let me be the angel at your tomb."

"You needn't bargain that way with me," he growled. He turned his back on her.

He marched out of the room.

That night he took a very long walk under the stars.

AS THEIR CARRIAGE PASSED through the country with the cross laid atop the baggage and tied down on the roof, people were waiting along the roadside for a chance to see the Christ, and perhaps to kiss his hand. Or so Sebastian believed until he climbed down at one small grove, a kind of oasis near a well where the crowd was particularly thick. He was wearing his black leather gloves, as usual, and had just begun to pull one off so as to let a particularly handsome woman enjoy the sight of his stigmata. But he stopped, seeing that she was looking right past him into the carriage window.

"Is it true, Cristo-Rey? Do you travel with the bride? The woman of the cross?"

He returned to the carriage and tried to be gracious, not to show how hurt he was. Assuming a playful tone, he said to Sidelle, "Well, my dear, they don't find me pretty enough. It's you they want to see."

The smiling coachman (a trainer of horses in the valley and an uncle of hers) helped her step down to greet the crowd. The cries that went up made Sebastian sit back in the shadow where the involuntary grimness of his face could not be seen.

Nearer their destination, there were other crowds that greeted her more solemnly, crowds of women especially; not his women, not the Magdalenes, though also dressed in black. Even in black, the Magdalenes were always dressed elegantly, with filigreed veils, ornately patterned, through which their adoring eyes could be seen to glow.

These women's clothes were dull black, often ragged, the same dresses worn for years on end in mourning. Sebastian was shocked time and again to see that many of them carried crucifixes of plain, unpainted wood, on which not he, not the Christ, but a woman, his bride, was hanging.

He could not get over it. Who had fashioned all these strange crosses? What workshop did they issue from?

The entry into the city seemed to take forever. She got out many times to let them look amazed at her hands, kiss them while sometimes moaning their sorrow. They were poor people, all of them . . . though why so few men?

They wanted to see her cross too. She and her uncle did nothing to stop the men and boys from climbing right up on the fender of the carriage to have a look at where her hands had been nailed.

Sebastian stayed hidden in the carriage with the curtain drawn on his side. He stopped peering out. He closed his eyes and went into himself each time she left him. He thought of other times when it was he who had stepped out to bless them. He had even gone to the trouble one year of memorizing a favorite passage from The Beatitudes. He had spoken the blessing given by Jesus Himself in a dramatic voice he had felt very proud of, the way it silenced the crowds by the side of the road, as if they expected him to perform some miracle right there and then. Indeed, he may have. He may have.

A leper had been healed. He had not believed it when he read it in the newspaper the next day, seated in the garden of the hotel where the guests could enjoy watching him out of the corners of their eyes. A blind man, the paper also said, had been given sight.

"I have no such powers," he had told a group of elegant ladies at the next table.

But perhaps . . . never mind.

The fresh breath of excitement she brought with her whenever she returned to the carriage was nothing he would begrudge her. The floor and the seat and even his own lap were filled with bouquets of wildflowers they had given her. Let her enjoy the notoriety. She had suffered for it. She was a woman deserving of spiritual awe.

He loved her body too, her flesh, her blood; he ached for the smell of her, certainly desired to have her bless him as much as anyone in those crowds, but to have her bless him more intimately, with her soft arms, her breasts and thighs . . . this radiant girl who had been crucified on the cross of the Cristo-Rey, who would lie in his arms come the resurrection.

Each time she returned to the carriage, and the horses lurched forward, she would give off a giddy laugh. She pretended to be mystified by her notoriety, but it was becoming clear to him that she had expected it, was prepared for it, and was even a little vain, he thought, explaining to him so proudly that all these women wearing and carrying their crucifixes with the image of herself impaled upon them . . . these dark, grimy women who had never appeared at his crucifixions, belonged to an order that had swiftly grown, she had just learned, from only a few, at the first meeting convened in a single small country hut, to several thousand, or perhaps even many more than that.

"Convened," he found himself saying. "It sounds more like a political order than a religious order. Next thing, they'll be asking you to carry on the rebellion in your father's place."

She thought about this for a time.

"It *is* an order to be reckoned with," she said.

These men and women smelled even worse than the people who came to the hacienda did, he wanted to say. Each time a mob of them converged upon the carriage, he had to endure their stink. Their shouting and shrieking had begun to hurt his ears too. He could not bear them, he was on the verge of saying.

But he managed simply to tell the coachman, between gritted teeth, please not to stop any more, he was suffering a terrible headache, to continue on as swiftly as possible until they reached the hotel.

He was sorry if he sounded cross, he told her. He was very tired. Depressed, too, by the sight of all the smokestacks belching out their dark spirals, the mountains of coal beside the factories, the blackened faces of the workers . . . the sadness, with only these strange women shrieking so happily when Sidelle passed. He had always regretted the coming of heavy industry to their once-beautiful country.

"It's *you* who should take my father's place," she said.

"Whatever do you mean, Sidelle?"

"I mean, to bring the land back where it belongs. A Christ is needed now."

He shrugged. "Render unto Caesar."

He pulled back the curtain, saw a whole long line of wretched women coming down a hill from a village of hovels. The woman who led them was being blown along by the banner she carried: a square, billowing sail of white satin on which was depicted in red a crucified creature of some sort, with broken wings and the head of a bird.

"What do they call themselves?" he asked. "Your women?"

She hesitated, pulled his gloved hand away from the curtain, and pressed it to her breast.

"They are *your* women too, my dear. Like your own kin, they call themselves *The Sisters of Sidelle.*"

ELEVEN

WHAT AN AFFRONT to call themselves *The Sisters of Sidelle*. They were not his women. They were not like his own sisters and aunts. Not at all. He was impatient to enter the more prosperous section of the city where he knew his own Magdalenes would be waiting. They were his, she would see. They were the ones who would want to kiss his hands and anoint his hair and feet. She would understand that he had his women too.

But it was dark when they reached the main avenue and turned onto the plaza. If they were out there, the adoring Marys, Sidelle would not have seen them.

He and Sidelle were given the bridal suite in a luxurious hotel impressively built of granite and marble, with a balcony where she could step through the French doors and go out in the torchlight to wave, to show her stigmatized hands to these mobs of poor women who had converged in such droves upon the city from every corner of the country. The tourists, the residents of the city, the visiting dignitaries seemed actually lost, so few they were among these Sisters of Sidelle, most of whom seemed to have left their husbands and sons at home. Sebastian looked at them through the shutters. He did not go out to join her. Perhaps he would later on. Let her enjoy their fascination with her wounds. He knew what the awe of the crowd felt like, how much pleasure it could give.

In three days, she would be his true wife. It would be good for both of them to have shared the love of the crowd. Meanwhile, his pulse was fluttering. He could hardly wait to settle in to his own ritual. Whatever strange new events were transpiring out there on the street, there was a certain kind of pleasure having to do with the night before his crucifixion that he was in the habit of enjoying here in these hotel rooms: a pleasure he saw no need of forsaking entirely.

It was the pleasure of making himself as handsome, indeed as beautiful as possible in front of the mirror, dressing in a sensuous and gallant way, and then going downstairs to the lounge, the dining room, maybe even to the bar, to be adored by his Magdalenes.

Would they be down there? Would he have time to enjoy, if nothing else, just the bachelor pleasure of remembering how he had given his heart to them before his marriage to Sidelle. It would not be unfaithful of him simply to bathe and clothe himself in a suit of fine white linen, to comb and curl his beard, to scent his hair and to brush it down in swirls over his shoulders, to wear a yellow silk scarf, his yellow suede gloves, his red Arabian sandals, to go down and, yes, why not? — to let them kiss his wounds.

While she . . . while Sidelle, so obviously awed and pleased as she had become with the goddess role her crucifixion had given her, received the adulation of this strange crowd she seemed to love; received the adoration of these women who felt they shared her crucifixion. He would enjoy one last round of the old pleasures while leaving her to her night of glory.

Or must he join her on the balcony? Was this the time to shock them with the image of the bridegroom Christ standing beside his bride? What would those who had come from abroad and knew nothing of Sidelle's martyrdom think of such a strange image?

No. For another hour or two, let her have them to herself alone. He would enjoy this fine hotel.

He had always looked forward to the hotel rooms where he was put up as a guest prior to his crucifixion. Invariably the finest rooms were reserved for him: a bedroom and drawing room like these, usually the bridal suite, where the odor of perfumes and bath soaps still lingered from the latest assignation.

Bridal suites were seldom wasted on brides in this country. It was considered unseemly for a woman of virtue to display too much sensuality. No, these bridal suites reeked of erotic play. There were always these paintings and carvings of fauns, nymphs, pink fleshed, voluptuously nude women sporting with some god or other; and of rococo cupids aiming their arrows at shepherd lovers, Pans with horns and furry tails lifting up goblets of wine.

It was known how the Cristo-Reys liked to be quartered in sumptuous rooms. A tradition going far back. Sebastian was always excited to be given a little time to indulge himself in such a place before the work began.

He ambled into the bath, sat on the closed commode and, placing his hands with satisfaction on the ornate brass handles of the tub (a mermaid and a priapic dolphin), opened the taps. He sat back and watched the steam rise, remembering the fantasies he had enjoyed (there was no harm in that) fantasies of inviting one and then another of his Magdalenes up to the room, sitting just where he sat now, lifting her crinolated black dress, all her black petticoats; placing his hands on the bare white flesh of her hips, above her black stockings, slipping his hands slowly upward, discovering with the tips of his fingers that she was already prepared to push his robe open and to sit on his lap facing him, her bodice torn wildly open, her bare breasts pushed against his chest.

No harm in fantasy. The dreamed and the real were entirely other. He knew that. He knew how to keep them separate.

It had been wonderful to arouse himself in that particular way before he had to go out in the sandals and white smock and purple robe of Jesus into the gloomy silence of Christ's impending death. No one could have expected him to hold to his celibate vow, even to the control of his fantasy. No, he had given himself full release over and over again, so that he might more meekly endure his trial, his long walk up to Calvary with the cross on his shoulder, the good and pious gentlemen of the town walking ahead of him carrying torches, their choir leading the way, venerable old men stopping frequently to sing the heart-rending dirges so that he might have time to rest the weight of the cross on the ground and look dolorously right and left, seeking compassion in the faces of the crowd.

On either side of him his brothers with their whips, playing the centurions. And, following close behind, the women in black, shouldering their images of Mary, their heavy palanquins, as he lifted the cross again and stumbled onward; the women of the aristocracy in the lead with their golden Maria, then the wives and daughters of the landowners with their Mary of gold and silver; the silver Maria next, and the one of painted wood . . . on down the line farther than he could imagine, there were so many who followed in his wake, from the very richest to the very poorest, each society with a Mary just as rich or poor as themselves.

Over his shoulder, he had never been able to see very far back down the line, except when he was near the top of the hill. But he had known them there, had seen them in his mind's eye, his Marys.

After, when they had lain their holy platforms down and had gathered around him at his cross . . . he had found time to look penetratingly into many of their faces, and draw courage. And he had seen into the eyes of every single one of them by the time they took him down from the cross.

But the ones he knew best were those aristocratic, worldly-wise women who had been able to afford the enormous price of being bedded for a night in the same hotel as he, so that they might catch sight of him, or even be kneeling at his feet when he indulged them with the slow, dramatic removal of his gloves and the display of his wounded hands.

Thinking of it while the bathroom filled with steam, he almost forgot to turn the water off before it overran the tub.

That was all over with. Why deceive himself?

She was the one they desired now. His wife. His virgin bride.

His Magdalenes had all deserted him.

No, that could not be.

He shed his clothes and dipped his toe into the water. It was still too hot. The porter had already placed Sebastian's small bag of toilet articles on a stand. Sebastian wiped the mirror with cold water, saw that his eyes had a slightly glazed look.

He realized that he was feeling betrayed.

By her?

No, not by her. By the people out there. They had forgotten him. He knew he should not be so envious. He no longer had the right to feel . . . what was this? . . . He could see it in his eyes. . . . Rejection? Disappointment? What else?

Jealousy.

Yes, a pitiful jealousy, of which he immediately felt ashamed.

He looked at himself wanly until the steam had clouded his face over, then got into the tub. With a groan of relief, he sank down into the water, letting the heat penetrate him to the bone.

He felt much better now. After he had dressed and admired himself in the many mirrors, he decided that it would not be such a bad idea to join her on the balcony just long enough for the people to have a look at him.

He opened the doors wide and stepped out into the balmy air and the torchlight. He stood beside her. He tried to take hold of her hand, but her fingers stiffened. He let go of them.

His appearance had silenced the crowd below—a crowd that he was surprised to see filled the plaza and jammed every street. Many carried torches. All eyes looked up as if waiting for some signal. Then one of the women began to hiss. She was quickly joined by others until the night was filled by that deathly sound, steady and continuous, the faces in the torchlight looking up, teeth bared, venomous.

Sebastian seized Sidelle's arm, pulled her back into the

room, pushed her so hard he sent her reeling against the wall. He shut the French doors and slapped the shutters down tight.

The hissing could still be heard.

"You mustn't go out there again," she said, recovering herself as she calmly opened a valise that had been set on a bench beside the vanity. She pulled out her golden angel costume and went to stand in front of the mirror, holding the dress up in front of her.

"Nor must you," he said.

"Oh yes, I must, Sebastian."

She lay the costume on the bed and began to remove her traveling dress. She had never undressed in front of him before, but she did so now without any show of embarrassment.

"Why must you?"

"Those are my instructions."

"Instructions from whom?"

"From my sisters. From my sisters and from yours. I must stand on the balcony as long as they keep coming."

She was pulling the golden angel dress down over her head. She looked at herself in the mirror, removed the combs from her hair.

He said, "I forbid you to go out there again."

She shook her hair out.

"My poor husband. The time has come for you to understand. For the Christ, it is finished. For us it has just begun. Before you ever reach your Golgotha, the crucifixion will be a thing of the past for both of us. It is already time for the annunciation. They have promised no harm will come to you."

"Who has promised?"

"Help me put on my wings."

She unfolded the wings on the bed, fixed the little snap hooks. He helped her strap the silver cords over her shoulders around her waist. She stepped back, wings outspread, smiling.

"How do I look, Sebastian? I'll go out now and put their minds and hearts at ease, you'll see. Before long, they will be singing. I'll stand before them all night long, and by the time the sun rises it may already be Easter. They'll love me. I'll make them want to sing, because this is the night when all of us will come down from the cross. I am so happy. I am so excited."

"Excited? Why? What's happening?"

"I cannot say. Truly, I don't know. I only know that it will all be changed and that I will teach them to love you too, I promise I will, and we will have our children and live happily in the valley of the Cristo-Reys."

"What are you talking about, Sidelle? What is this babble of yours?"

"Ah, Sebastian," she beamed, "you do look so dashing. But it would be best if you did not come out onto the balcony. Now, open the doors for me. I'm going out."

H E   L E F T   T H E   R O O M and went downstairs. The lounge was full of military men. There were no women there.

On his way to the dining room, he was stopped in the corridor by an exhibition of copper plate etchings. They depicted the disasters of Napoleon's recent war with Spain. In one image, two French soldiers had hung one of their enemies from the limb of a tree. The limb was too low. The soldiers had seized their victim by the ankles, lifted him up, and were tugging at his legs.

A white whiskered gentleman in a military uniform, who had just strolled out of the bar, stopped beside Sebastian. He, too, studied the picture.

"It's not easy to break a man's neck, is it, Cristo-Rey?"

Sebastian realized that here was none other than the Supreme Commander of the Emperor's Military Forces, the very one who, at Sebastian's trial, had wanted to have him shot.

The Commander's tone was friendly enough, though, when he asked what Sebastian thought of Goya.

"Your father once told me he disliked Goya for having taken the beauty out of war," the Commander said. " Strange notion for a Christ to have."

"I know little about art or artists, Commander. I only remember that my father compared Goya unfavorably to . . . who was it? A certain Greek."

The Commander rolled his eyes. "Ah well, yes, the pious Greco! With him there's none of this pushing and pulling on the horizontal plane, is there? I could never make your father see the beauty of any kind of action that takes place beneath the horizon. He was like my wife that way, if you'll forgive so ludicrous a comparison. Ah, look at this one."

Sebastian joined the Commander in front of an etching that showed a peasant in a white shirt torn open at the breast, wild haired, wild eyed, up against the wall, his hands raised in a helpless gesture of self-defense as the soldiers of the firing squad fired away.

The Commander nudged Sebastian. "Just between you and me, there'll be a lot of hell breaking loose very soon. The more go down, the better, as far as I'm concerned. It was you who got all this started, wasn't it, Cristo-Rey, if you'll pardon my saying so. Innocents like you always unleash this kind of chaos." He lifted a finger, almost touching it to Sebastian's nose. "And then it's people like me who have to bring it under control. Do you know where I'd like to see you when it happens?"

Sebastian was feeling so disconsolate that he answered almost with yearning: "Against the wall, I presume."

"Now, is that a nice thing to say? No, not at all. I want you to have a better view than that. The best view of all." He lay a comradely hand on Sebastian's shoulder. "I'm hoping you can observe the entire battle while you're up there on the cross, dear fellow. You'll make a fine distraction, too, for the women to enjoy while we men play out our little scene of gunfire and brimstone down in the pit."

" I'm afraid I don't—"

The Commander patted Sebastian on the back. "It's all such theatre, is it not? Goodnight, Cristo-Rey. I'd advise you not to linger in the bar. There's a drunken woman in there whom you'll find quite obnoxious. I regret that she happens to be my wife."

The Commander's face had suddenly reddened. He pulled a cigar from his beribboned pocket, bit off the end, spat it on the carpet, and marched away. He was swallowed up inside the dark red cavern into which the gaslit hallway receded.

Sebastian proceeded to the bar.

THIRTEEN

THOUGH IT WAS already late, Sebastian was surprised to see only men in the bar, and not the sort who usually stayed at his hotel for the sake of their wives. Every one of these men was in the uniform of an officer. Judging from the way they glanced at him with such contempt, he certainly did not want to join them.

Where were his Magdalenes?

Usually during the Lenten season, when so many thousands of women invaded the country, the more elegant hotels–especially the hotel where the Cristo-Rey was staying–cordoned off special areas for women who felt compelled to drink, as most men of their class did, even during Holy Week.

But there seemed to be no women gathered together here, sipping at their drinks and speaking gloomily of spiritual matters while they waited, hoping the Christ would come sit with them.

He had just turned to go back to his room when a woman's voice called to him hoarsely:

"Cristo-Rey!"

He spun about.

Seated in the shadow cast by the overhanging leaves of a philodendron, in a black leather chair, wearing a black dress and a huge black hat, the veil lifted, a white faced woman with painted lips motioned with her black gloved hand for him to come join her. In front of her chair and the chair next to hers was a table with two brandy snifters on it, hers almost empty, the other full.

As he approached, he was pleased to see her push herself

forward off her chair, down to her knees on the carpet. She reached out pleadingly for his gloved hand. Embarrassed that the men were watching, Sebastian nevertheless was thrilled to be enjoying the familiar adorations of at least this one–this first of the Magdalenes since he had arrived in the city–finally to be treating him as so many of them had in years past. And she, so stunningly attractive in a dissolute, sultry kind of way.

He had no compunction about giving his hand to her and standing there while she turned her head sideways, stared up at him with a tragic eye, shook her hair loose so that it fell over the glove, brushed her hair adoringly over his hand, then seized him by the wrist with one hand while pulling at the fingers of his glove with the other. She got the glove off and pressed her cheek imploringly to his wound.

He bent forward, trying to hide how powerfully aroused he was. He let several intense moments pass before he withdrew his hand, placed it on her head, brought it firmly down her hair, around to her chin. He lifted her face so that they could gaze deep into each others' eyes with a practiced spiritual rapture. Standing up so brazenly straight that he caused her eyes to flutter with what they saw, he brought pressure on her chin, lifted her to her feet, and watched her fall back limply into her chair with a contented sigh.

"Oh, Cristo-Rey," she cried softly, "I knew you would come if I waited here long enough."

She pushed her hair back from one eye, and looked at him quizzically. "You do remember me, don't you? Last year I met you in the arboretum. You allowed me certain discrete pleasure that I will always feel grateful reliving. How could I have forsaken you? No, no, I could not have."

She was so much the very type of the women who adored him: matronly, yet sensuous, slightly hysterical, yet with a worldly wisdom, a sorrowful forgiveness in the eyes. There had been so many last year in the lounge, the dining room, in this bar, in the hallways, and, yes, in the arboretum, that he could not remember which one she was. More correctly, she was all of them.

"It is I who feel grateful to see you again. Believe me, Madame."

"You do remember me, don't you, Cristo-Rey? Melisande Gonzalez de Sevilla. You raised me to my feet there amidst the fragrant gardenias. Remember? You blessed my name."

"Indeed."

She clasped her hands. "I have followed you and your father to so many places. It feels strange finally to have you here on my own territory. And at such a time, when all the others have forsaken you, some of them even to becoming sisters of that detestable order, even to the outrage of taking you down and putting her there on the cross in your place. Where is the world going, I ask you. Come sit down. Explain all this to me."

Seeing him look toward the corridor, she reached for her brandy, swirled it around.

"Don't worry about my husband. I know you must be tired of hearing what the men have to say to you. But he's gone for the night. Off into some remote corner of this hotel, you can be sure. With his concubine. We do not share the same room, or even observe the amenities for very long, you see. This time his excuse to throw a scene was that I drank the brandy. I gulped it when I should have sipped it."

She sat bolt upright, made a double chin, and spoke in her husband's voice: "Sip it, Melisande. This brandy was sent to me by the great Bonaparte himself. It survived great storms at sea. Sip it! For God's sake, just take a little in your mouth at once, just a vapor on your tongue, Melisande. For God's sake, don't *drink* it."

She fell back with a guffaw. The officers at the bar turned to look. This only made her speak louder.

"I said to him, 'Hernando, my little man, your Melisande will sip what she sips and drink what she drinks.'

"Oh, la-la! I'm sure he was still performing his petulant

theatrical when he passed you in the hall. Here's his drink, untouched, you see. Do come sip away at what the big emperor sent our little emperor from Versailles. Or do you abstain before going to the cross?"

"*Au contraire, madame.*"

Sebastian was still standing there, uncertain whether to sit down.

She signaled for the waiter, who brought the bottle, and filled her glass. Sebastian looked about. He saw that there was really nobody else to converse with.

He searched into her face, trying to understand what it was about the particularly ravaged beauty of the Magdalenes that so stirred his lust: A look? What kind of look? A look of passionate yearning for some vague kind of erotic union with the mystical, some final union with the image of Christ earned through years of anxious and restless indolence, and perhaps sexual disappointment.

"I'll sit with you for just a little while, madame."

"Well!" She pressed her hands to the swell of her cleavage. "So. Here I have you next to me. How different you look, all dressed up, as it were."

Teasingly, she unfastened the top clasp of her dress, pulled out from between her powdered breasts a silver crucifix, on which he was relieved to see that his, and not Sidelle's, effigy was affixed.

He watched her rub his image between the thumb and forefinger of her gloved hand, giving his stomach even more of a polish, and then his loin cloth, and his legs. All the while, she grinned in an obscenely suggestive way.

Her lower lip curled downward, displaying its wetness. "Poor me, my Christ is in such trouble."

She let the crucifix slip down into the darkness between her breasts.

"Oh, how the gentlemen are distressed with you."

"Are they?"

"Who can blame them? First you steal the hearts of their women, then you bring about the loss of that one pleasure their sex knows how to enjoy. From the very heartland of the Cristo-Reys, you somehow let this rebellion get started. And now it flares up all over, and dies, and flares up again. Congratulations. My husband says that you are a disaster as Cristo-Rey. Do you know what I answer back?"

She leaned forward, narrowing her blackened eyes.

"Indeed he may be, I say. But I am a loyal woman. I have wept at his cross since I was a girl. Am I to stop weeping now? When I was little, my grandmother was already taking me to weep for his grandfather. Then it was his father. And now, what do you expect? He may not be as great as certain legendary Christs of the past. But, as you so often say, the world is running down. And I continue to adore the man, if only out of habit. Out of religious laziness, I worship him, though what you say may be true. He may have lost his vital contact with the true Christ of our fathers. What can I say to that? He is, nevertheless, in my blood."

She placed a hand on Sebastian's knee.

He looked at it there, and was about to lift it off, and give her some kind of firm indication that she should not act familiar with him in this way, with the soldiers glancing over their shoulders.

But he was remembering how Sidelle had spoken to him in their suite, so coldly, and with a frightening, almost arrogant confidence. The memory of this made it especially delicious to feel his Magdalene's hand sending a current of warmth up and down his leg. He decided to let her hand continue smoothing its way up and down his thigh, while he attended further to this monologue of hers.

"I am not very kind when speaking of you, Cristo-Rey. But I could show you a way of loving that would please you . . . if you had the courage to let yourself experience it."

Her hand pressed close to his groin. He did take hold of her

wrist now, with the tips of his fingers, and place the hand back
in her lap, though gently, and with a subtle pressure against
her own thigh, before he let go. He crossed his arms over his
chest. He cleared his throat, as if he, not she, were the one
who was speaking.

She continued in almost a despairing voice: "I love you with
all my heart. That is the bitter truth. Close up, you thrill me
more than any singer or soldier or matador, even though I
know you are not truly he. When I gaze at you up there on the
cross, you send chills up my spine. The world seems to begin
and end with you, horrible as you may be. You've brought
about the ruin of my kind of people, there's no question about
that. Still, I won't desert you, as have the other women of my
class. It's more than a rebellion. A real revolution's brewing
this time. You seem not to care. There in your valley, you even
encourage it. Don't think we weren't on to you. This country
is well equipped with spies. I could curse you like the others
and merely tolerate you for the attraction you still hold among
our guests from abroad. Across the seas, you are still the most
famous person in our country. People risk sickness and ship-
wreck just to see you crucified. I could curse the irony of that.
But I continue to sing your praises here in my breast.

"I shall be up there at your cross again this year, with all the
foreigners. Our own will be hidden in their houses until this is
over with, I can assure you. But I? Melisande? Your most faithful Magdalene? I shall be there, looking up at you, whatever
the danger. And when they take you down–God willing–I shall
perfume your body; I shall wrap it in winding sheets, my dear
bridegroom. In sheets of white satin. Even if I have to do all
the lifting and turning by myself.

"Mind you, I have even seen to it that you will spend three
very comfortable nights in the tomb. The soldiers will carry
you there. Real soldiers, Cristo-Rey, no butchers or bakers or
men from the market dressed up in Roman costumes, but real
soldiers, I assure you. Because you'll need real soldiers to

guard you from some of the *grands seigñeurs,* whose hench-
men will be waiting along your path. You'll need protection
from the rabble too, for they also have a score to settle with
this Christ who raped their queen."

Seeing how his eyes had clouded, she placed a hand this
time more tentatively on his shoulder, patting him lightly.

"There, there, calm down, my poor Cristo, my gentle Jesus-
Jester. The rabble will be taken care of by the time they're
pulling the nails out of your fists. And then I'll have our soldiers carry you to a beautiful little temple with a door as strong
as you'll find in any prison. Nobody can break in, you'll see.
You'll be safe and sound in there until the angel comes. No
dark, putrid tomb this time. Oh, the holes you Cristo-Reys
were laid in some times. How did you ever come out of them
alive?

"But this: this is the mausoleum of my own esteemed family
you will be laid out in. And when you've unbound yourself,
you'll find that I've put warm clothes and blankets and everything you'll need for your toilet. And a quite comfortable
couch. And plenty of provisions: food and wine, and even a
few troubadour romances, if you read that sort of thing. Or you
can read the inscriptions on the caskets of my ancestors: the
first man of my family who landed here with the conquest to
capture the Indian gold; and the next, who chopped down and
sawed the first of the forests; and all the others who planted the
standard of Christ on these predestined shores and claimed
what this land had to offer, through God's providence. You
will see their very uniforms and faces carved in marble above
their tombs. You'll even be able to study the strange beauty of
the thick veined hands the sculptors immortalized unto my
own grandfather's elegant, long fingers crossed over his heart,
God rest his intrepid soul. He was the one who dug the very
hole under the hill of your Golgotha from whence our salva-
tions will storm forth and bring down the end of the pagan
world.

"I'm breathless. I'm babbling. I should say no more.

"Shhh! Do I speak too loudly? Never mind. Those boys are on our side. Where was I, Sebastian Cristo-Rey? Yes. There, inside our mausoleum, our dear Lord and Savior can have himself a very pleasant time, too, reading on the plaques how the women of our family stood by their men, God save their skulls.

"Read, rest, there will be plenty of light. A grilled window in the door through which you'll smell the blossoms this time of year. You can even look out and catch a few glimpses of the battle, if it's still raging.

"You look surprised, Cristo. What battle, eh? No, no, I cannot tell you that. My husband would nail *me* to the cross."

She nodded toward the bar, lowered her voice.

"We're on to them, though. That's the thing. There won't be one of them left alive by the time we're through. Oh, what a wailing there will be among The Sisters of Sidelle! Pardon me, I don't mean *your* sisters. They'll be spared, of course. Why shouldn't they have gone insane for a time, after what they went through. Let them return to the old ways, and they will be forgiven. I mean all those others and their virgin empress.

"Your unwanted bride! Have no fear. We'll take her down from the cross this time. You'll be rid of her before we're through. That I can promise you.

"What? I can see that she hasn't told you a thing.

"She means to betray you, Cristo-Rey.

"Aye, aye, aye, aye! The poor man! Look how his eyes grow large! He hasn't been informed? They really do despise you, don't they? How miserably they have treated you, and for something anybody could see was not your own doing? Of course, you did take the girl against her will. Do you think I was not taken against my will? I was given to my husband by arrangement, as with any other barter: like gold or cattle or lumber or so many tons of coal. But to dishonor a man who gave them back their land? You would think they actually believed the ones who say that it was you, my poor, timorous Cristo-Rey, who nailed her to the cross. As if it were just too inconceivable that a father could do such a horrible thing.

"Do they think we women never tell one another what crimes our fathers committed against us? The Cristo-Rey would never punish a girl that way simply for refusing him, I said. Have you not seen the man? I have spent hours looking up into his face. I know his soul, Sires. I know his very blood and bones. I know the beauty of his flesh, I could have added. The way it shines. No, no, trust my intuitions. The girl was done in by her own kind. Peasants are that way. They're beasts, forever needing to be put back in their place, retamed. Her father was the spoiler!"

She brought her hand away from Sebastian's shoulder. Leaning forward, she covered her face with both hands. It was hard for him to hear what she said. He had to lean toward her.

"When I think that you were forced to marry that wretched girl, who surely hates you, and thinks . . . *thinks* she'll have her revenge. Doesn't she? Taking your lead: dividing up the land, returning what was claimed by the throne, by divine right . . . returning land, so hard to clear and cultivate, to people who have no notion of how to manage an estate. Parceling it back to anyone who kneels down before her throne and claims that the land once belonged to his family. And what if it did? Back then, there were nothing but trees. It had never occurred to these savages that they could clear land, till, and plant, irrigate, and nurture. Well, let's just wait and see. I've told you more than I should. Too many eavesdroppers at the bar."

She uncovered her face, and glared at the officers, who quickly returned to their drinks.

"Look at them, so happy to know there's soon to be a great bloodletting. That's what all men love, isn't it?

"You smile. I thought so. The old ways suit you better, don't they, Cristo-Rey. A good bleeding. That's what a noble señor like you longs to accomplish in the springtime. No more of this forced marriage to the daughter of the beast, heh? Oh, and don't think our dear archbishop hasn't written to the Holy See to tell about the desecrations of your family church. Dear God! Where did she get such power over you? Well, we always knew that you were weak. We saw it in that long face of yours, yet loved you for it, being weak ourselves.

"Never mind. You and all our men will emerge from this stronger than ever. A real resurrection! I'm of the old school. Such a rejoicing you're going to see when this is over, Cristo-Rey! When the troublemakers are dead and the natives are back where they belong.

"The fiestas we've planned! Oh, what a merry dance we'll have when you push back the stone this time! The Emperor and his consort are coming from the capital with all their court. Everyone of importance will be here, once the city's made safe again. Tomorrow, perhaps. As early as tomorrow, if we catch them tight in the net."

She finished off her drink, sat back, studied the ceiling where a pastoral scene showed a blue gartered courtier seated under a tree with his eye on the peasant lass who had turned from amidst the sheep to show him her blushing smile.

Melisande Gonzalez de Sevilla shook her head.

"What astonishes all of us is that they should attempt something so bold. As if they stood a chance. Surely they must know there isn't a single tribe that doesn't have its spies. Not a single guild or lodge. Do these poor simpletons really imagine that our Emperor and his generals do not know why so many men are missing from their work? Why so many peasants have left their fields? Where *are* these men, heh? Tell me that.

"You have no idea, do you, Cristo-Rey?

"They're all around the city, champing at the bit, ready to ride. Out there over the hills, hidden in arroyos, in caves, God knows where.

"And, tell me, has that chieftain's daughter whom they call your wife . . . has she informed you? Oh, my, my, my! Do look at his face! He thinks his Judas wife doesn't know. She, whose father was the leader of them all. She could have saved our lives, and even now while she stands out there in the wind watching the whole herd of them — thousands upon thousands, I'm told, and still stampeding into the city from all sides to have a look at her — she knows. She *thinks* she knows that her husband and all the rest of us are doomed.

"Has our dear Sidelle of the wounded hands told you that your own body is the signal: that when the people see you raised up on the cross, there on the great hill under which the first coal tunnels were built, the first mine opened up . . . when they look to the top of that hill and see your cross go up, with you hanging upon it, and all The Sisters of Sidelle — that is what they call themselves, you know — all the sisters of your bride Sidelle surrounding you, holding off anyone who would try to save you . . . has she told you how, with the signal that you, the Cristo-Rey, have given up, and I mean *truly* given up the ghost, they'll ride in howling, firing off their guns? They'll ride in from the countryside and make an easy capture of this city? And the women will cast aside their veils and black rags? And reveal themselves dressed as brides for the resurrection of the goddess? Has she given you even the slightest hint?

"No? She has told you none of this?

"Or is it that she really doesn't know.

"My, my. He looks so wounded. His Melisande was being cruel. Of course, the virgin wife could not be told. Why should they risk all by informing her, just because they plan to make her their queen. Their virgin mother. Their Tree Empress, yes!

"Just because she is as clever and wily as her father.

"Jesus the Cristo. So wide-eyed. Just look at him. My fisher of men.

"You see, the thing is, the Commander-in-Chief has gone fishing too. He wants them all in his net this time. It could be over in a few hours if there's no hole for them to slip through.

A slaughter is so swift when executed well . . . Oh, my, forgive your Melisande. I had forgotten your brothers. How cruel of me.

"I should not say another word. It's time for bed-bed. This has been a most interesting conversation."

She set her glass down.

"And now, my dearest Cristo-Rey, would you be so kind as to accompany one who remains faithful to you to the end—"

Sebastian's ears were ringing. "Accompany you where, madame?"

He wiped a cold sweat from his forehead.

She winked. "Why, to my room."

FOURTEEN

SHE STOOD UP, took his arm, and walked with him unsteadily into the hallway, casting such a withering glance toward the soldiers at the bar that they all lowered their eyes.

He tried to hurry her along, but Melisande Gonzalez de Sevilla would not be rushed. She stopped in front of one of the Goya etchings.

"Read it to me," she said. "I'm half blind in this light."

The etching showed a woman in her bridal gown, seated at a vanity, with a grotesque woman of skull-like face hovering behind her, saying, *"Hasta la muerte."*

"Until death," Sebastian said, feeling a chill in his hands and feet. "One of the *capriccios*, I believe."

"Yes, death, Cristo-Rey. For you, it's all part of the act, isn't it. A mere whimsy, a family tradition played out on the cross. Capricious indeed." Melisande pressed her body against his. "But Goya wasn't drawing a man's preparation for the cross; he was drawing a woman's preparation for a much more ghastly scenario: the wedding ceremony." She heaved a great sigh. "Cristo knows nothing of a *real* marriage, does he? A real marriage means a real death, you can take my word for it."

The blast of brandy fumes in his face reminded him of Roman when his brother had been drunk and boasting of his conquests. She licked her lips.

She said, "Speaking of the whimsical, have you ever kissed one of your Magdalenes?"

He grabbed her firmly by the elbows, straightened her up. She got control of herself. She walked with more dignity beside him now.

Her room was around a corner on the same floor, through a maze of mirrored pillars and waiting rooms, beyond an isolated alcove where a liveried servant, a white haired old man, was standing at attention by the door.

"You must come in, Cristo-Rey." She tugged at Sebastian's sleeve. "I have so much more to tell you."

"My wife is waiting for me." Sebastian pulled her hand loose, bowed, and kissed it politely.

The servant had opened the door to reveal a room with a red canopied bed. She said to him, "Anselmo, are you informed of where my husband is just now?"

"Certainly, señora. He is with one of his ladies."

"And where is the wife of this gentleman I'm with?"

"Wife of the Cristo-Rey, señora? Why, showing her presence to the crowd. They say she is standing on the balcony in the appearance of an angel."

"When will she leave the balcony?"

"They say she will not, señora. Certainly not for very long. The crowd is enormous. More are arriving all the time. They fill the main streets of the city, and have organized themselves as a procession so that they can walk past to receive her blessing."

"Her blessing for what, Anselmo?"

The old man frowned. He pressed his lips tight together. He rubbed his hands on his breeches.

Finally, he murmured, "Not for me to say, señora. Not for the likes of me to say."

"You see how discrete he is," she said to Sebastian. "I can assure you that if you come into my room nobody will be the wiser. And I have so much yet to tell you. If my Cristo-Rey is very, very good to me, I will tell him just what surprise my husband has in store for Sidelle and all her so-called sisters and brothers. Don't all men love to know the battle plan? Surely you're no exception."

"Then tell me now, Melisande."

She gasped. "You spoke my name. Oh, Sebastian, do come into this chamber that I have reserved in secret now these many months, just for you. Just to fulfill my dream. Am I not your Magdalene? Am I not your ever-faithful one? Surely now that it is almost over, now that it is nearly ended, we should finally claim our right to know each other."

"It is very late. Tomorrow—"

"You know nothing of tomorrow, my poor innocent. This is our only chance. Don't tell me you haven't dreamed of it? Haven't I read your eyes for hours on end? We must do what we have always known that we must do. Now. Tonight. Or we may never have another chance."

She saw his shoulders fall. She seized him by the arms. Passionately, fiercely, she glared up at him. She shook him hard.

"Tell me you haven't loved me in all your many Magdalenes. You have, I know you have. Just as I have loved you in all the images of Christ. Yet, when have you dared to know me in a single one?"

"I was vowed to celibacy, and then to marriage."

"Marriage as a punishment. So was I. That is not marriage. You need not keep your vows to a woman who, even tonight, is plotting your death on the cross. And I, Sebastian, whom I can finally call simply by his given name: I have loved you in so many thousands of images of Christ, yet never known you in a single one. How many times in my life have I not knelt until the pain shot up from my knees into my womb? How many times have I not longed to press my hands to your ribs, to your loins, to lay myself across your crucified body. You belong to me. Whomever you have been wed to, you are *my* bridegroom." She wrinkled her nose. "And, behold, the bridegroom cometh."

She pulled him into the room.

The servant pressed the door shut behind them. The lock was heard turning. Sebastian leaned against the door, his hands flat against the wood.

She stepped towards him, crushed her body against his.

"Don't you know how I have suffered your wounds, as if they were my own? Don't you know how I have lain my body against yours on the cross, day after day, night after night?

"Have I not earned the right to ask you now to be amorous with me? I am the last. All the others have deserted you. Look, there on the vanity. A note from my daughter. I told her I was determined to see you. And do you know what she said? Slut. She dared call her mother a slut. She said, 'Very well, then, give him this.'"

Melisande pushed away from Sebastian. She strode to the vanity. She snatched up her lorgnette, unfolded the letter, and read: "Dishonorable Sir:"

Melisande looked up at him bitterly. "You understand, this is from a woman now twenty-two whom I once bore in my womb."

"Read it to me," he said.

"Dishonorable Señor:

From the time I was a little girl, I had cause to be afraid of men. They were all after possessing me. My father, my brothers, my uncles, the men who moved through our home. The soldiers had more than their eyes on me. Whenever they got a chance, they had their hands on me as well.

And so I am afraid of them. Yet in need of a good man, and as attracted to what I hoped a man could be as any other woman.

What I loathed about the men I actually knew is that they could seize me at will and render me helpless. They could do with me as they pleased. With the images I saw of Christ, it was not that way.

His hands were nailed to the cross. I could look at him, lust after him day and night if I pleased, and there was nothing he could do. He was pinned down. Just as I, being cursed by beauty, had been pinned down so many times.

I could remove some of the pity from myself by pitying him. I could even pity him that he could not touch me. Finally, I began to wish, just because he could not, that he would.

And so, he became the man I yearned for, even after I was forced into marriage. More so after I was married to that fat, grunting swine I was supposed to take my pleasure with. I closed my eyes when my husband had at me. Instead of him, I saw your long, slim, naked torso. Your melancholy eyes, Cristo-Rey.

Yes, after I was given in marriage, I felt somehow the wounds given to me as a bride, a woman, a mother, when I bore my greatest pain, were the wounds of Christ. What he had taken into his hands and feet, I had taken into my body. I suffered his wounds as I suffered my own. I longed to console him as I myself longed for consolation.

He was my lover, my secret husband.

And you were he.

You were he for so many of us.

Now you have betrayed us. I detest you.

You have come down from your cross, and nailed me to it in your stead.

You have brought a huge desolation to my heart. To the hearts of all my sisters.

How could you have done such a horrifying, cowardly thing to me? To all of us who loved you and lived for you, believing you to be different than all the others.

We hereby abort your vile person from our hearts.

Never again will we weep at your cross."

Melisande Gonzalez de Sevilla crumpled the letter. "Though she signs herself 'A *Sister of Sidelle*,' she is my own daughter. She wrote this in behalf of all your women. All your women, except for one. Except for me, her tragic mother."

"But it was not I who nailed her to the cross," Sebastian protested.

Melisande threw the letter to the floor. She returned to press up against Sebastian. "I am your last, yes. Your only one. Feel this body of mine? Did you not look down from your cross and claim me as your own? Or was I deceived?"

"But who are these women who believe that I would nail my own bride to the cross?"

"Of course it was not you. Heaven forbid. No, no, no. It was her father, you poor misunderstood Cristo. It was her father who did it for you. I understand perfectly. Let's blame it all on her father, shall we, my poor, innocent Prince of Peace. Or wait! Still better! Let's say it was the harpist. Because . . . because, you see, you could never have done this yourself. You made him do it for you. Or was it *your* father? The sublime Abraham, Master of Sacrifice. Whoever did it for you—" She was giggling against his chest, her voice smothered. "Left you quite innocent."

She raised up, and said meanly, almost spitting in his face: "Just as God is innocent."

They breathed in unison against each other while Sebastian thought about this.

Then his hands came away from the wood, and found her perspiring back, her hips, her buttocks. He pulled her hard against him. She leaned back, looked up, saw him close his eyes, saw his head turn.

"No, my Lord," she moaned. "Do not turn your face away. Not any more. I could not bear it. Look at me. Carry me to bed looking into my eyes. I want you to look directly into me, and I shall look directly into you . . . until we both have died to everyone and everything else."

He picked her up, and carried her. He lay his Magdalene down in the red shadows, where he could break the little clasps, and spread the darkness apart.

"What are we going to do to her?" he said, as calmly as he could. "How are we going to defeat her?"

"I have told you."

He forced a smile through the infinite sadness he was feeling.

He pretended to gloat: "The battle plan, Melisande."

"Afterward." She was panting heavily. "Afterward, you will know. But, for the love of God, can't you forget all that for just another hour? Cristo-Rey, I want you to take me. Take me as you do your virgin brides!"

He closed his eyes.

He saw her.

He saw Sidelle lying on the cross. He saw himself seizing one of her hands, holding it down on the beam with his knee, taking the spike from his mouth.

While he was seeing himself raising the hammer and pounding in the spike, Melisande unfastened him. She reached inside. Taking hold of him with claws, she guided him into her most ardent wound.

Over and over through the night, they devoured each others' agony, until they both cried out in a final plea for mercy . . . and then fell upon each other, descending into oblivion, through spirals of increasing blackness, down, down, holding fast while they fell, and let go of each other, and spread their arms, pressed hands against hands, fingers stretched out. . . .

And they surrendered; they gave up their ghosts; they died for an uncertain time.

He awoke. She was sitting up, leaning against the headboard. A cupid on the bedpost shot an arrow at him over her shoulder.

"Now," he said, trying to sound contended and casual.

"Now?" She smiled at him. "Sebastian, my own, how good to see you looking so utterly at peace. No more the man of sorrows, heh? Now . . . what?"

"You were going to tell me the battle plan. I simply must know how we are going to put a stop to these vermin."

She smirked. "I confess, I tricked you. I could never."

"If we are to be what we are to be . . ." He rolled onto his side away from her, pretended to pout. "We must have no secrets from each other, Melisande."

She lay there trying to resist. But she couldn't help the chuckling, then the laughter . . . until she was sitting up, eager to declare: "Oh, my prince, it's so very cunning."

"You say cunning?"

"Cunning, cunning, cunning. I should know. I was the one who thought up the strategy. We women are much wiser when it comes to setting traps, you see. I said to him, you'll see, my little commander in chief. You'll see that your Melisande is not quite so useless after all. She knows you men for the sneaky little boys you are. Oh, how you love to creep up on each other. Well, your Melisande, Señorito, is going to show you how to have some fun!"

FIFTEEN

"OH, HOW THEY LOVE their Trojan horses. How they love surprise! Do you know where his boys are now? A whole battalion of them, with their horses and their cannons? No? You can't guess where? Under the hill. In the mine shaft under the very hill you chose to be the high point of your drama, your precious Golgotha. We've hidden half our army under there. My husband's a clever scoundrel once I get his brain to working.

"He'll let the rebels take the town, you see. Right during your crucifixion when nobody's expecting any harm. Except to you, of course. To our dear Cristo-Rey whom everybody will forgive. I'll see to that, once our troubles are over, once he's been set free from the power of the witch."

She tugged at his ear.

"Set free," Sebastian said. "Yes, I'll be set free."

Melisande chuckled cruelly. She pulled the blanket over him and smoothed it down on his back.

"We let them all ride in, my lamb. We let them set up their barricades and guns, whatever they have . . . it doesn't matter. We'll let them ring themselves in. We'll let their leaders storm the palace, if that's what their hearts desire. Let them ha-rangue whatever crowd deserts you and scurries down from Golgotha to listen. Let every traitor burst out of his house to cheer. The more the merrier. We want to catch them every last filthy one of them.

"Meanwhile, what is happening outside of the city? Heh, my little Cristo? I'll tell you what. Out there on the hacienda which I and my husband and our dear children usually call our home, believe me it is no home to us just now. We are all here at the hotel, tucked away in our sinful little rooms, each to our games. My children with their nanny, my husband with his whore, me here with my Cristo-Rey. And our house? The stables? The outbuildings? The granary? Even the chapel? Our hacienda has become a barracks, a hiding place for the other half of my clever husband's army.

"The half that surrounds the city, do you see, *Sebastionito*?

"Ooooh!" She threw a bare leg over his. "Look how huge my Jesus' eyes have grown? He's just beginning to see the strategy. The Christ is starting to understand how generals think! Yes. Exactly. We put a ring of cannon and of riflemen around the town. And then . . . then, from the center, from under the hill, alleluia, long live the shortest lived revolution of all time! From the center, from under crucifixion hill, the gates fly open and the fiends ride out!

"Rather brilliant, what? If I do say so myself?

"If you've hoped to avenge the rape of your sisters, that will be the time. And your hands will be clean, Master Peace-maker, you may leave the bleeding to us. Now, now, calm yourself down.

"Long live our goddess, they'll all be crying, waving the banners and crosses of the female Christ. They'll think our army is still two days' march away. Plenty of time to loot and kill and—first, of course—before the bloodbath, to take turns cheering their revenge against the bleeders of their women and their land. They'll be up there making proclamations from the balconies . . . when . . . oh, my dear Cristo . . . can't you just see the way their leaders cry out with surprise? What? The doors of the mine—

"The doors of the mine have flown open! My husband's finest troops, his cavalry come galloping out of hell, right down the central esplanade where the rebel forces are all still crowded into the plaza, cheering.

"Flee!"

She cried it out hoarsely, her forehead turned against Sebastian's shoulder.

"Run for your lives! But where? Look. They've encircled us inside and out. The reign of the goddess is over before it ever began. And we? Oh, my Sebastian darling! The land is saved for those to whom God gave it in your name. Praised be spirit of the Archangel Michael. Hold high the sword of the conquering Christ. Above all, glory to my husband, the Napoleon of the New World, and to His Empress! *Vive les Grands Seigneurs!*"

SIXTEEN

HE HAD EXPECTED to find Sidelle still out on the balcony, but she was seated on the floor with her arms wrapped around her knees. One wing, broken from her shoulder, lay beside her on the carpet.

The French doors were shut, but the crowd could be heard out there chanting her name.

She lifted a tear streaked face.

"I cannot bear it," she said. "They want too much."

He knelt at her feet.

"What is it they want?"

"I do not know," she whimpered. "I am told nothing. To appear. To appear in front of the people, they say. What is it all about, Sebastian? What am I doing dressed as your angel if I am to—"

"If you are to be my *avenging* angel?" He smiled wanly. "If you are to announce my death on the cross?"

She seemed genuinely startled.

"Oh, no, Sebastian, I would protect you. Truly, you are my husband. You have been good to me. Oh, please, tell me what to do. If they would harm you? No! Then I would refuse to play any role in their drama. I told them so. And they understand. If they intended to harm you even in the least, let them find someone else, I said."

"But you seem to be enjoying all this adulation."

She lowered her head to her knees.

"I'm frightened," she said. "I'm very frightened."

"Could it be that you don't know what's happening, Sidelle?"

He pulled away her other wing, picked her up, lay her down on the bed. "Do you really not know, my dear bride?"

She shook her head.

He could see that it was true. The queen bee was quite innocent of what the drones were up to.

"Who does know?" he asked gently. "Is it a man? Your leader? Who leads your army? You must tell me."

"I know nothing of armies."

"Sidelle, I'm not asking for my sake, but for yours."

"I will not let them do you any harm. I won't! I won't!" she wailed, and rolled over clutching the pillow.

He waited until she had stopped weeping and had turned on her back to look at him, studying his face.

"This is all too difficult, Sebastian."

"Now you must listen to me very carefully, my angel, because I am your only hope. The imperial army knows every detail of the uprising. The plan is for all of your people to be slaughtered, and for you to be burned as a witch. Only I can save you. So you must tell me."

"But tell you what? What am I supposed to know?"

"Surely you know who it is I must speak to if you are to be saved."

She leapt from the bed and walked quickly to the French doors. Parting the shutters, she stood for a time peering out.

"You really do hold me dear, don't you Sebastian?"

"I treasure you. Though I must confess to you, Sidelle, that I have lost all right to your love. I deserve nothing but contempt from you."

"That is a very weak thing for a man to say."

"Then give me a reason to be strong. Tell me who has instructed you in all this."

She looked at him over her shoulder, and threw up her hands. She spun around.

"My uncle," she blurted. "You'll find him in the carriage house. Go tell him quickly. It's already dawn."

SEVENTEEN

H E W A S S C O U R G E D with real whips during his trial in front of Pilate. A real crown of thorns was forced down on his head. Real stones were thrown at him along the route to Calvary. The Roman soldiers handled him roughly when they nailed him to the cross. Somehow, Sebastian survived it all, exhilarated finally to know, as he looked up to heaven, that he had earned his suffering, and that his naked, bleeding body was the signal for the country to die and to be born again. Through his love for Sidelle.

He began to scream.

He was glad for the rage of these women when they looked up at his agony and shook their fists. He bared his teeth. He screamed even louder.

The mob of women howled up at him, taunted him while they showed him their crosses large and small. Crosses with dolls of all sizes dressed in wedding gowns and nailed to the wood . . . this mob whose earthen, ravaged faces had come up from a ground he knew not of. He was glad that he could bleed for them, could howl back at them with genuine pain.

Glad that he could roar out his laughter when the mountain shook, when his cross trembled and swayed and left him looking downward, tilted forward on the place of the skull, atop the ravaged hill. He was glad that he could shriek at the women as they ran so terrified, so horrified, down the hill; they retreated up through its rubble again to form a tight, clustering circle around his cross, still not aware that the victory was theirs, that half the imperial army had been trapped inside the galleries of the mine where, even now, those soldiers, servants of the mighty, were gasping for breath in the smoke, dropping their weapons, falling from their horses, and giving up the ghost.

Now he felt the rumbling. His cross shook and swayed time and again until it was almost uprooted from the ground. He was leaning far forward now, the nails tearing at his hands.

But he held on. He could not let himself die while there was this terrible scene to observe. He screamed with joy, and he screamed with horror as half the imperial army died inside the mountain, sealed in by the rebel troops, entombed. And look. He shrieked at the sight of it, far off there beyond the city, the rebels had the hacienda surrounded. The Commander's men were trapped there too.

"Bravo!" he sang on his cross. "The king is dead! Long live the queen!"

When the smoke had cleared and the Sisters of Sidelle finally understood that the victory was indeed theirs, they abandoned the cross, and hurried down the hill again to see their empress and to walk behind her warbling their victory cries as she was paraded through the streets.

His Roman soldiers were not there to take him down. A band of peasants carrying rifles and wearing bandoliers pushed his cross over until it fell on top of the Christ. His protests were shut off by a mouthful of dirt.

They pulled the nails from his hands, untied his feet, and carried him over their heads through the mob, down to the tomb that had been prepared for him. He was thrown in there unconscious. The door was locked. His captors hurried away to proclaim the good news to the celebrants: it was finished.

The Cristo-Rey was in the tomb. He would not emerge on the third day. The angel of his annunciation belonged to the people now. He would stay in the tomb until he died.

The bleeding was over. Cristo-Rey would never rise again.

EIGHTEEN

NO ANGEL APPEARED at the doorway of the tomb to announce to the Marys the resurrection of their Lord. The wealthier Marys were hiding in their houses with their husbands and their children, or fleeing in their coaches toward the borders, or to the sea.

Those among the poorer Marys, who had run over to the tomb to peer in at the bloody, unconscious Jesus lying there naked between the stone sarcophagi, did not linger long, for they knew that the Angel of the Lord would not appear to announce Christ's rising from the dead.

Their angel had been installed on the throne by a new government of the people, which had toppled the church, and restored the old religion.

The shouting of Sidelle's holy name, the victory cheers, the blowing of trumpets, rolling of drums, exploding fireworks, were all so loud that Sidelle could not have heard the regular salvos from the rifles of the firing squad as row after row of men and women from the aristocracy were lined up against the wall across the road from the cemetery, and shot.

They were still being shot when Sebastian awoke, and staggered to look out his barred window. He wondered when the bandoliered peasants, who were guarding his door, would unbolt it to announce that his turn had come.

It never did.

That Easter Sunday, and for weeks to come, he watched the gaily dressed people rush up and down the streets. They sang, they caroused, they celebrated their victory by sometimes running in droves to the tomb to take turns one by one looking in at the window while everyone screamed out mockery of the defunct Christ.

The food and clothing Melisande had said she would leave were not to be found. At first, he was obliged to be seen with only a bloodied cloth around his waist. But eventually he was given a few changes of clothes and his purple robe.

After the first few months, when the throng had dispersed, and the men and women of the revolutionary army had returned to their homes, life seen through his window appeared relatively calm again. People who came to peer in at Sebastian no longer spat or cursed; they simply stared at him with morbid fascination, trying to imagine how this tall, bearded gentleman in his regal robe could have nailed their empress to the cross.

Women guards, as fierce and militant as any men, wearing uniforms even more braided and bejeweled than those worn by the soldiers of the deposed regime, were posted night and day on either side of the door to make sure nobody attempted to shoot him or to break in, and to keep him from breaking out, since he was a real prize, a legend who brought wealthy visitors to the city.

He learned from the guards that, in deference to his being the husband of their empress, he would be decently clothed and fed, but he would never be released. He was to be punished for his crime against her by being kept in the tomb until he died.

Melisande Gonzalez de Sevilla appeared once at his window with another woman. They were both dressed in widow's black.

"I wanted you to see that we survived your betrayal," she said. "This is my daughter. Come, darling, look at the worm of God."

"Devil!" the daughter screamed.

"Oh, yes," Melisande said wearily. "We do hate the Cristo-Rey with such a passion. Do we not?"

He turned away, and crawled behind the stone casket of one of their ancestors. He stayed hidden there, enduring their curses until they were gone.

Not all visitors were unfriendly.

A few took special pleasure in speaking affectionately to the Cristo-Rey, as if one so evil as he could endow them with a special feeling of goodness for being out there in the sunlight on the other side.

He was kept informed about events in the world by his guards, though what he saw most often, when nobody happened to be looking into his cage, had to do with death.

The sepulchre in which he lived was on a grassy knoll, just inside the entrance to the cemetery. It was a temple-like building of imported marble with beautiful stone angels—he was told—standing atop the columns at each corner, blowing trumpets.

Visitors who had come to look at the infamous Christ were not allowed inside the cemetery during funeral services, so the burials became a welcome respite to Sebastian from his being on display.

The funeral processions entered the gates, and moved directly towards him, turning up one or the other flowered path to right or left, just before the iron fence encircling his hillock.

It was still the custom for someone carrying a crucifix to lead the way, though Sebastian could see that now the effigy on the cross was that of a woman.

Behind the crucifix, the priestess walked, swinging a censer of smoking cedar chips. The fragrance reminded Sebastian of times when the wind had blown down through the forests above the valley of the Cristo-Rey. He could breathe in deeply, close his eyes, and pretend that he was standing on the porch of his home, looking out toward the orchards and vineyards.

The most evident influence of the old religion on the new

was that the last person walking in the funeral procession—usually an old woman—carried a sapling, holding it by the trunk, the roots wrapped in wet sacking. A tree was always planted now at the foot of a grave.

Indeed, Sebastian learned, the planting of trees had become an important ritual since Sidelle had become Empress. During her brief reign, her major influence would be in bringing about a reforestation of the country. Sebastian learned that she had introduced an old custom: before a priestess performed the wedding ceremony, the couple first pledged their troth to the tree of their choice, as a sign of their enduring love and care for the natural world.

Sidelle was apparently used by the government as a mystical symbol. She had become a religious figurehead, to be paraded about on ceremonial occasions, and to preside over holy days. But, otherwise, she was kept hidden in the cloister of her country residence, where the Sisters of Sidelle attended to her needs, there in the valley that was no longer named after the Cristo-Reys, but was called *The Valley of the Virgin*.

So that the mystery of her presence not be diminished, she was never allowed to speak or to appear at secular functions. Political proclamations were made in her name by whomever happened to have established authority over the revolutionary junta that year.

At first, the government was entirely in the hands of women, and many women had even joined the military. But the country to the north, a Christian monarchy, began to test the strength of its neighbor with border incursions. When these were successfully repulsed, more men were brought into power.

Three years after Sebastian's entombment, the women guarding his tomb were replaced by a single friendly young man, from whom Sebastian learned that the junta was gradually returning power to the new landholders, and to an emerging mercantile class. The junta was made up now of an equal number of men and women. Women, Sebastian's guard assured him smugly, would soon be back in the home where they belonged.

By the following year, this seemed to have happened. Though, once a year, at the vernal equinox, a huge religious event took place in *The Valley of the Virgin*. All the men from the palace arrived in their carriages to pay homage to their Empress, and to join the pilgrims who filled the whole valley. Barefoot, they escorted Sidelle, followed by all the pilgrims, up the hill to the living tree upon which she suffered herself to be nailed while the people prayed and sang.

During his seventh year of imprisonment, a letter was passed through the bars by an old woman who had recently set up a fruit stand against the wall across the street from the cemetery.

The letter read:

> My Highly Esteemed Husband,
>
> Though neither I nor your sisters are permitted to communicate with you, I write this through the help of Talifiero, my harpist and now my scribe, hoping that she whom I most trust will deliver it to you. It is to inform you that your father is dying.
>
> Know that I am as much a prisoner of my father's religion as you were.
>
> I am never allowed out of here, except to be carried around seated on a palanquin, a kind of throne.
>
> Great crowds still come to see me crucified every year, even though a perpetual Easter was declared when I first ascended the throne. There is talk among the sisters of moving my crucifixion to a large city where more tourists would be attracted from abroad.

The influence of the Christian church is hard to dispel. There is also talk of a compromise. We would be crucified side by side, or back to back. Upon a tree, of course. Upon a living tree.

It has been hard for people to return entirely to the old religion. Compromises must be made, I am told.

I wonder if anything has even been gained in my name. There is more gentleness in the land, to be sure. And, except for me, women are more free to choose how they would live. Also, the forest will some day be thriving again, thanks to what my worshippers have done.

My scribe is not a worshipper. He merely loves me. He wishes to say what I would never allow him to say if I could read what I have begged him to write, or if I could guess that he is making this discreet addition to my letter.

I have borne him two children in secret. A boy and a girl. Your sisters, Maria Sidelle Dolores and Maria Sidelle Inez, have claimed them as their own. But their father and I remain their true guardians. Be assured that neither of them will ever be taught to worship a god who hopes to save the world by the torture of his favorite child. Neither of them will be offered up as sacrifice for anyone's sake. Their hands are clean and clear. They bear no wounds. They know no grief. And we pray they will be of no grief to anyone else.

Though I have my children and my throne, my scribe wishes to say that I am most unhappy. He will tell you honestly: I have suffered continually all these years to think that you would sacrifice so much for me. Daily I weep for you. I beat my breast. Sometimes, thinking of you, there in your perpetual tomb, I tear at my hair, and cry out to Our Lady of Mercy, in whom I claim not to believe.

My scribe wishes you to know that I love you in a way so profound and mysterious that he cannot even comprehend it. He can only wonder, and despair, and testify as you already know that singers must.

Know, then, that your Sidelle will continue to plead for your freedom. She says she would rather live in the tomb with you than in this house without you, where she will surely die of a broken heart.

Your wife, faithful forever in her love,
Maria Sidelle de Cristo-Rey

After he had received this letter, people who came to look in on Sebastian's cage would find him standing in the middle of the room, the letter clutched to his throat while he sang at the top of his voice, and while the men and women carved of stone lay on their tombs to either side of him, hands folded over their hearts, apparently listening.

The singing of the Cristo-Rey was eerily beautiful, and finally frightening. For he would not stop. Refusing food from his guards, taking only water, he sang night and day, until he could sing no more.

Shortly before he died, the woman from across the street was allowed into his cell to see if she might persuade him to eat and drink. He was lying on the floor, arms spread, his eyes closed, scarcely breathing.

The woman got down on her knees. She put her ear to his chest.

"Is he alive?" the guard asked.

"Hush."

The woman patted Sebastian's cheek until his eyes fluttered open.

Calmly he looked at her.

"Who are you?"

"Look, I bring you wine from the vineyards of the Cristo-Rey."

"I know your face, woman."

"This bread is from my oven," she said tenderly. "I have added some healing herbs that were grown on land you once owned. Take. Eat. It will make you well."

"I have seen your before."

"Yes, a few times. You have. But you have never known me."

"Are you . . . ?"

"I am your mother, Sebastian."

The Cristo-Rey lifted his head. His mouth opened wide.

The guard who heard it said he gave off a last long cry, like an infant left alone in the dark.

"Like this," the guard said. "Like a lost calf.

"Maaaaaaa!"

EPILOGUE

THAT SAME YEAR, the brief rule of the goddess came to an end. The country to the north finally received the help it needed from a large industrial power to conquer its smaller neighbor.

Sidelle was nailed to the sacred tree, and burned as a witch. Talifiero fled with their children to a safer land.

The true church was restored. Old Abraham Cristo-Rey was not as near to dying as Sidelle's scribe had made him out to be. The old Christ was found still alive in his hermitage, and was persuaded to play the sacred role until such time as Hilguero, the son of Maria Latona, whom Abraham had initiated with the stigmata, should be old enough to take his place on the cross of the Cristo-Rey.

Hilguero Cristo-Rey proved the greatest crowd pleaser of all his lineage. He married, had four sons, and assured the survival of the tradition right up to the time, late during the last century, when public crucifixions were finally banned.

On certain of the more remote haciendas, however, the bleeding of the virgins by the *Señores* is still practiced. Though, in most parts of the country now, it is only the land that continues to be bled.

ABOUT THE AUTHOR

PIERRE DELATTRE is the author of *Tales of A Dalai Lama, Walking On Air,* and *Episodes.* He has published stories, poems and essays in many magazines. From the time he received his graduate degree in the sacred arts, Delattre's interest has been in moral and spiritual aspects of contemporary culture. During the 'beat' era, his coffee house in San Francisco's North Beach was a gathering place for poets, actors and musicians. He has worked in radio, theatre, television and film. Delattre lived and taught in San Miguel de Allende, Mexico, for fifteen years, aligning himself with the 'magical realists' both in writing and in painting. As a painter, he manages his own studio/gallery in Truchas, New Mexico where he also holds salons and workshops on the relationship between the arts and the spiritual disciplines. He lives in the foothills of the Sangre de Cristo Mountains with his wife, the painter Nancy Ortenstone. Pierre Delattre can be contacted via his website: *pierredelattre.com*